MURDER CLOSE TO HOME

MURDER CLOSE TO HOME

A Brother Dominic & Detective Miller Mystery

JAMES M. MCCRACKEN

DEDICATION

To my cousin, James Martin
who encouraged me to continue
writing about Charlie and Howard.

CONTENTS

ACKNOWLEDGMENTS

A special thank-you to Dennis Blakesley, Rita Waite,
Roxsee Huff, Tamera Somers, Micheal Anne Maslow,
Anthony Huff, Pamela Cowan, Cynthia Ley, Emma Chavez,
and to my fellow authors of the Northwest Independent
Writers Association (NIWA) for their continued
encouragement.

CHAPTER ONE

Brother Dominic MacCready stood at the head of the classroom and looked at the young faces of the boys seated at their desks. He glanced to his right at his reflection in the glass doors on the large bookcase that sat against the wall. His unruly auburn hair and red beard were neatly trimmed. His ears that once seemed to stick out a little too much, somehow no longer did. His grandmother, Ophelia, always told him he would grow into his ears. The thought made him smile and turn back to the class.

He still couldn't believe that just a handful of years ago he was the student sitting nervously in class on the first day of his freshmen year of high school. It didn't help that the old neo-gothic brick building that was Saint Michael's Abbey looked like something out of a horror movie, but in time these boys, his pupils, would become used to it as he had. Some may even decide to make the Abbey their home.

"Good morning, my name is Brother Dominic. I will be your English teacher this year. I know you have all had a chance to meet each other, but if you would be so kind as to stand and introduce yourself, I would greatly appreciate it."

One by one the ten boys stood and said their name,

some quickly sitting back down, others confidently and slowly taking their seat again. Brother Dominic made mental notes.

"Thank you," he said. Turning around he took a book out of his satchel and pulled the desktop lectern closer. He then sat down on his desk and held up his book. "I believe you all have a copy of this book?"

A few boys responded with a muffled, "Yes, Brother." Others simply nodded their head.

"Good. Please take them out. This will be one of the textbooks we will use this year."

No sooner had the boys taken out their books when the classroom door opened, interrupting them. Everyone turned and watched as the school principal, Brother Simon, a tall, gaunt monk with a more sinister than holy look, walked into the room. He appeared to glide across the floor in his long black habit as he went straight to Brother Dominic. Dominic quickly stood up. Brother Simon whispered something into Dominic's ear.

"Very well," Dominic responded. He returned his book to his satchel. Turning around, he looked at the boys who stared at him with puzzled expressions as another monk walked into the room.

"I've very sorry. It seems I've been called away. Father Anthony will be taking over for me. Please show him the same respect and courtesy as you have shown me." He picked up his satchel, nodded politely to his replacement, and followed Brother Simon into the hallway, closing the classroom door behind them.

"Are you sure about this?" he asked while he walked down the hallway on the second floor of the abbey building.

"I'm afraid so," Brother Simon answered. His tone was very serious, almost stern, and his words short and to the point. "Abbot Ambrose was very clear. You are to come to his office immediately."

"Do you know what it's regarding?"

Brother Simon stopped and turned to face Dominic. The expression on his face said all that needed to be said.

"Never mind," Dominic spoke.

"One doesn't ask questions," Brother Simon said. "One does as he is told."

"Yes, Brother Simon," Dominic said. Suddenly he felt as if he were back in high school being disciplined by his dorm overseer.

"Don't just stand here, be on your way," Brother Simon said before returning to his office.

Dominic hesitated a moment while he collected his thoughts before turning around and heading to the monastery wing through the door at the opposite end of the hallway. His room was on the second floor with a view of the cloister garden behind the abbey. If he hurried he could drop off his bookbag and be downstairs and no one would be the wiser.

He rushed across the mezzanine above the foyer and through doors to monastery wing. His cell was near the end of the hall. He opened the door to his small room and turned on the light. His single bed sat against the wall on the right, directly in front of the door. A small table with a lamp served as both a nightstand and side table to the overstuffed chair that was in the corner against the wall on the left. Above the table was a window that had a view of the cloister garden below and in the distance, Black Butte, a small mound south of the abbey. Between the door to the private bathroom on the left and the entrance door was a large, heavy, antique wooden desk. Dominic set his bag down and quickly left his room.

A moment later, out of breath from hurrying, Dominic stood in the hallway outside Abbot Ambrose's office on the main floor of the students wing. Having a familial connection to someone at the abbey was comforting when he was a teenager and it remained that way as an adult. But that didn't stop the butterflies from beating their wings in his stomach while he waited for his grand-uncle, the Abbot, to respond to his knock.

"Ave," came the response from inside the office.

Slowly, Dominic turned the doorknob and opened it. Inside the office, the wall behind the Abbot's desk was completely covered by a large, oak bookcase. Most of the shelves were filled with books of all sizes and in all genres. Dominic was certain his grand-uncle had read them all. On the few shelves that were void of books, potted plants filled the space. A heavy oak desk sat in front of the bookcase and faced the door with its edge against the wall to the right. A small, pottery, oil lamp with an acorn stopper that held the wick sat burning on the corner of the desk away from anything flammable.

Abbot Ambrose sat in his chair behind the desk. He looked over the top of his half-moon spectacles at Dominic without his usual smile.

Dominic opened the door wider and stepped into the office. His right leg brushed the chair that was set against the wall in front of the desk. He glanced to the left as he closed the door behind him.

The left side of the office was set up for relaxed conversation, if one could relax when speaking with the head of the abbey. A stained glass floor lamp sat behind a small side table with a rounded top. Two, ox blood, leather winged-back chairs were set on either side of the table. Dominic recoiled slightly when he saw one of the chairs was occupied by a young man, about his age. He recognized him immediately. His name was Samuel Coffey. They met a month ago when their mutual friend, Cody Jacobson brought him to the Abbey on a visit. But something was off. Samuel was wearing a torn, short sleeved shirt, dusty and grass stained denim jeans and he was barefoot. His feet were covered with dirt. Dominic looked at the abbot.

"Please, have a seat," Abbot Ambrose said, gesturing to the empty chair beside Samuel.

Obediently, Dominic sat down but couldn't help

looking at Samuel. There was something odd about him beside his clothes and lack of shoes. His eyes stared blindly, straight ahead. His cheeks were covered with dirt that was streaked with tears. There were bloody scratches on his forearms as though he had run through a briar patch. His shirt was torn and snagged.

Dominic looked at Abbot Ambrose. "What happened?"

"I don't know," he answered. "He hasn't spoken a word since he arrived a few minutes ago."

Dominic turned back to Samuel. "Sam, what happened?"

Samuel didn't flinch. He continued to look at nothing, seemingly lost in his thoughts.

"Please, look at me," Dominic said. He reached across the small table and put his hand gently on Samuel's forearm.

The moment Samuel felt the touch, his body jerked and pulled away. For the first time he turned and looked at Dominic. His eyes were wide with fear. Then he turned back and stared straight ahead.

"He's in shock, I think."

"I've summoned Brother James from the infirmary. He was with a patient but said he would be down as soon as he could get away."

Dominic nodded. "Should we call the police?"

"No," Abbot Ambrose said. "He's come here for sanctuary. Until we know more, we will look after him."

A knock on the door drew Dominic's attention away from Samuel.

"Ave," Abbot Ambrose called out.

The door opened and a tall, grey-haired monk with a long grey beard entered the office. In his right hand he carried a black satchel no bigger than a lunchbox.

Abbot Ambrose motioned with his right hand toward Samuel. Brother James, a nurse practitioner, knelt on one knee in front of the distraught man. Placing his bag on the floor he opened it and took out a penlight. He began to examine Samuel's eyes without touching him. He took out his stethoscope and gently pressed the round knob against Samuel's chest. He didn't react.

"He's definitely in some sort of shock, though he doesn't appear to be severely injured. I need to get him to the infirmary," Brother James reported. "Can you stand?" he asked.

Samuel didn't respond.

"I need you to stand up," Brother James said, rising to his feet and stepping back.

Surprisingly, Samuel stood.

"I'll take him to the infirmary and get him cleaned up and checked over. I'll let you know how he is as soon as I can."

"Thank you, James. Take good care of him," Abbot Ambrose said.

Dominic watched the two leave the office before he spoke. "What do you suppose happened?"

"I don't know," Abbot Ambrose said.

"Do you think—"

The telephone on the abbot's desk rang, interrupting Dominic.

"Hello," Abbot Ambrose said into the receiver. "Yes.— I see. How long will you be needing him?—I see. You're absolutely sure you can't handle it without him?—Very well. He'll be waiting for you when you arrive." He lowered the receiver, placing it back in the cradle of the telephone. He took a deep breath and turned back toward Dominic. "That was Detective Miller. He is on his way here to pick you up. Seems he needs your help on a case."

"My help?"

"Yes. I'm just as surprised as you."

"What case?"

"He couldn't say. He just said it's important and he needs you."

"For how long? I have my classes."

"For as long as it takes. Father Anthony will continue to cover your classes."

Dominic's eyebrows pinched above his nose as he tried to imagine why Howard would need his help with a police matter.

"And son," Abbot Ambrose said, pulling Dominic out of his thoughts. "Not a word about Mister Coffey."

"Yes, Abbot Ambrose."

"You can wait for him in front."

"Thank you," Dominic said before leaving the office.

The lobby of St. Michael's Abbey and Seminary building was plain. It's walls were painted white. The white marble floor glistened in the light from the large, brass and crystal chandelier that hung from the ceiling. Each wall had a set of doors. Heavy wooden doors across from the glass, outside entrance doors led to the Abbey Church. The doors to the abbey wing were to the right of the entrance and the doors to the students wing were to the left. Dominic imagined from above the abbey resembled a capital E with the legs pointing south and the spine facing north.

While he waited, he began to pace. His thoughts went back to his first day walking into the abbey. He was a mere boy of twelve. That was nearly seventeen years ago. So much had changed since then but a lot still remained the same. Howard Miller was the first friend he had made and they were still close friends. After their freshman year in the seminary college at the abbey, Howard decided to transfer to the University of Oregon Law School and study criminal law.

Gustav Kugele, or Gus as everyone called him, was another close friend. After only six months of college he transferred to Oregon State. After he graduated, he moved to Seattle to work for a startup company involved with something called computer technology.

Rick Walters, another high school friend, left Saint Michael's after his sophomore year and moved to a small town outside of Lafayette. He joined a Trappist monastery there. Now known as Brother Conrad, he writes a few times of the year but the Trappists are a contemplative order devoted to silent reading and prayer along with manual labor. Each year, at Christmastime, Brother Conrad sends Dominic one of the Trappists' fruitcakes made with the nuts and fruits grown on their property. And each year, Dominic gave it to his grandmother. He didn't care for the candied fruit bits or the taste of rum that permeated the ring cake but his grandmother and her friends at The Towers seemed to love it.

Dominic smiled to himself. After graduating from high school, he used the money his father had left him to move his grandmother into the retirement home at the base of the hill across the street from the abbey. She was hesitant at first, saying that the money was meant for him, but he explained that as a monk, he had no use for it, and besides, there was plenty. Once she was settled in her new apartment, she seemed happy again. She and Howard were the only two who still called him by his birth name, Charlie.

Across the Great Lawn Dominic spotted a black Lincoln Town Car approaching. He walked outside and stood beneath the portico. When the car made the last turn and headed toward him, he walked down the front steps to the sidewalk.

The car came to a stop in front of him. Howard turned off the motor and stepped out from behind the steering wheel.

"Nice car," Dominic said before Howard could speak.

Howard glanced at the vehicle and shrugged. "It's the department's." He looked across the hood at Dominic with a somber expression.

Charlie's eyebrows pinched above his nose while he did a once-over of his best friend as they both walked to the front of the car. Howard was dressed in a dark, navy blue suit, white shirt and black necktie. His dark, curly hair was trimmed short. He looked as if he hadn't shaved that morning but he was just heavily whiskered with a permanent five o'clock shadow. Howard had traded his heavy black rimmed glasses for a silver grey wire rimmed pair. Even with the slight tint in the lenses, Dominic could see Howard's eyes were red and tired.

"What happened to you?"

"Don't ask," Howard said. "I should have been a monk."

"Another late night date?"

Howard scowled at Dominic. "I wouldn't call it a date. It was more like a wrestling match. She being the aggressor and me trying to get away."

Dominic let out a laugh.

"Oh, it was not funny. Nothing is more off putting than, shall we just say, an amorous drunk. I finally got away from her when she passed out. Then I had to take her home at three in the morning."

"I'm sorry. So, you won't be seeing her again?"

"I didn't say that. She's fine when she's sober," Howard said with a grin.

"So, what is so important you had to drag me out of my classroom?"

"Didn't Abbot Ambrose tell you?"

"Not really."

"We got a call a few minutes ago," Howard said. "A possible homicide in an old farmhouse. It's my first one since making detective."

Dominic made the sign of the cross. "I see, but what's that have to do with me?"

"I wanted my best friend with me. After all, you helped me study for the exam. You all but took the detective exam yourself."

"That's bogus," Dominic said.

"No, it's true," Howard said. "I couldn't have done it without you. Besides, I think we may know the victim."

CHAPTER TWO

The drive out to the farmhouse on Meridian, a two-lane country road, didn't take long even with Howard driving at a respectable speed. Dominic stared out the window at the fields and trees. The leaves on some had already begun to change to their bright yellows and reds of autumn.

"I don't think I'm ready for this," Dominic muttered to himself.

"Ready?" Howard asked. "None of us are ever ready to see a murder scene."

"No," Dominic said, turning to look at Howard. "Fall. I'm not ready for the season to change."

"Oh, for crying out loud, Charlie. Focus."

"Yes, sir, Detective Miller," Dominic said with a smirk.

Dominic noticed a small cluster of trees ahead. As they drew nearer, he saw a farmhouse on either side of the road. Howard began slowing down. Dominic noticed flashing lights coming from behind an overgrown laurel hedge by the house on the left. Howard passed the driveway and turned up another one just past the hedge. He stopped behind a patrol car.

Opening the driver's door, Howard stepped out of the

car. Slamming the door shut, he walked around the vehicle to the passenger side.

Dominic stepped out of the car and, as he shut the door gently, he glanced over his shoulder toward the street. He spotted a couple standing in their front yard on the opposite side of the road. They were staring at the house behind Howard.

"What's with them?" Dominic asked.

"Gawkers, I suppose," Howard said and held out his hand with a pair of blue latex gloves. When Dominic didn't respond due to looking across the street, Howard nudged him in the shoulder. "Here, put these on," he said, "Just in case you get the urge to touch something."

Dominic took the gloves and started to slip them on. "Don't worry, I won't touch a thing."

Howard looked past Dominic at the couple of gawkers. "We'll talk to them later. First, let's go inside to see what we have." He started for the front door.

Dominic turned around and for the first time really looked at the old, weathered siding on the farmhouse. It appeared to have been neglected for many years and was definitely in bad need of painting. The front of the house with its raised porch was shaded by a large oak tree. Another tree just as big was planted on the west side of the house opposite the driveway and shaded the house from the scorching afternoon sun.

"Come on," Howard said standing beside the police car with the flashing lights.

"I'm coming," Dominic responded. While he walked up the driveway he noticed the overgrown laurel hedge that shaded the driveway and the east side of the house, it also obscured the view of the neighbor's house. Like everything else, it too had been neglected. In front of the squad car and parked next to the house was an old, battered, red pickup with two flat tires. Dominic picked up his pace to catch up with Howard. He was almost to the front porch steps when something stirred in the tall weeds that was once the front lawn. Dominic jolted but quickly recovered when he saw a group of three chickens roaming freely, pecking and scratching at the ground. They appeared to be undisturbed by the commotion of the police cars.

Dominic followed Howard up the wooden steps to the front porch. The weathered and worn floorboards creaked and felt unstable. In some places the wood had either worn or had rotted completely away. Dominic felt his anxiety grow in the pit of his stomach. He followed Howard inside.

Upon entering Dominic was struck by a familiar musty odor. Memories of his attic bedroom at his grandmother's house on Tam O'Shanter Drive came flooding back. He shook his head to refocus on the present. The narrow entry was made even narrower by stacks of old newspapers and magazines that were piled chest-high against the wall on the left. On the right was a small table covered by a thick layer of dust. Past it was an open door. The living room, while in the same condition of needing a good cleaning, appeared to have been used recently. Dust covered the back of the old sofa, but the seat was clean. The same with the upholstered rocking chair. An old, portable television with crunched up balls of tin foil on the ends of the rabbit ear antenna sat on a cart in the corner next to a fireplace. Dominic noticed the partially burnt log in and cold embers in the firebox. Beer bottles, red plastic cups and food containers that weren't completely empty covered the coffee table and spilled onto the floor.

"Police!" Howard announced while they stood in the foyer looking into the living room.

"In here," a man's voice called from the back of the house.

Dominic shook off the feeling of ick and followed Howard down the narrow hall. He didn't notice the staircase against the left wall until they were beside it. Like the foyer, there were stacks of yellowed newspapers and old magazines piled higher than the risers and partially obscuring the stairs.

At the end of the narrow hallway, two open doorways faced them. The one on the left, Dominic could see, was to a bathroom. The other was to the kitchen. Howard entered that room.

"What are you both doing in here?" Howard asked. "You're supposed to be securing the scene, that means the outside, too."

"I am—we are," the younger officer answered.

"Then why's the house not taped off? Who's making sure no one is disturbing the property while you're both in here?"

Dominic stepped into the doorway and noticed two officers. One stood directly in front of Howard, the other was standing in front of the sink.

"Uh, I'll get right on it, sir." The young officer, a rookie, said.

"While you're at it, turn off the lights on the car. No need to kill your battery."

"Yes, sir," the rookie said. He slipped past Howard and hesitated when he saw Dominic. "Excuse me, Father," he said.

Before Dominic could correct him, he was gone. Dominic returned to the doorway. Howard had moved across the room to beside the other officer.

With an unobstructed view, Dominic noticed the small kitchen table in the corner across from the doorway. It was beneath a window with faded red and white gingham curtains. Two chairs, one with its back toward the door, the other to the right of it with its back toward the wall, were at the table. On the table, Dominic saw two wine bottles with wax candles. One had burned down to the mouth of the bottle, the other had been knocked over and the flame extinguished. There were two place settings of a paper plate, a plastic fork and a knife set in front of the two chairs. Unopened takeout boxes of food from Dragon Fountian

Chinese Restaurant in Silverton sat waiting in the center of the table along with two unopened fortune cookies.

Dominic looked at the floor beneath the table. A broken wine bottle with what looked like a puddle of red wine lay on the floor with the shards of glass. The whole scene gave him the impression that the table had been bumped sharply or shoved.

Dominic took a step into the kitchen and stopped. He looked at the officer standing across the room in front of the sink.

The officer stared at Dominic.

"What's—"

"Ignore him, he's with me," Howard interrupted. "What did you do in here?"

"Nothing," the officer said. "I just picked up the chair and put the dishes that were on the floor into the sink."

"Were you sleeping the day they taught you about securing the scene at the academy? You're not to touch anything. You're supposed to leave the scene exactly as you found it until the detective arrives." Howard looked under the table and then around the floor. "What else did you touch?" he asked.

"Just this." He handed Howard a plastic bag he picked up from near the sink. Inside was a black leather wallet. Dominic noticed the officer's bare hands.

Howard let out an exasperated sigh and snatched the bag out of the officer's hand. "You're supposed to leave things as they are until the photographer has taken pictures of the scene?" he grumbled, shaking his head in disgust. Looking at the bagged wallet, he asked. "How did you pick this up?" He carefully removed the wallet and opened it.

"I used the plastic fork that was on the table," the officer answered.

"So, you didn't touch it?" He looked at the officer's hands.

"No, sir."

"Brilliant, the plastic fork is now useless," Howard said. He reached out and took the pen from the officer's breast pocket. "Next time use this." He pressed it flat against the officer's chest. "And you might try putting on some rubber gloves." He glanced at the wallet again then looked at Dominic.

Dominic was staring at the body on the floor. He quickly made the Sign of the Cross.

"Are you okay?" Howard asked.

Dominic nodded but continued to look at the body. The young man was lying on his stomach with his head pointed toward the back door. Even with the amount of blood that soaked the victims shirt, you could tell he was wearing a dark blue, green, and gold plaid shirt, untucked. His blue jeans were old and faded, and he was barefoot.

Howard began to make notes. "A male victim in his mid-thirties—"

"Twenty-eight," Dominic corrected him.

The officer gave Dominic a curious look and then looked at Howard.

"Short, brown hair. About six foot. A single shot to the back between the shoulder blades." Howard closed his small notebook. He removed the wallet from the plastic bag and opened it. Carefully he took out the driver's license. "Humph," he grunted and held it out to Dominic. "Have a look at this."

Dominic took the license. "Samuel Coffey?" he said, sounding surprised.

"Do you know him?" the officer asked, eyeing Howard and Dominic with dissaproval.

"Yes. He's a friend but…that isn't his wallet," Dominic said nodding toward the body on the floor. "This is Cody Jacobson."

"How do you know that?" the officer asked.

"We both went to high school with him," Dominic replied.

"You did?" the officer said and looked at Howard.

"You can wipe that look off your face, Officer. We weren't friends, at least I wasn't his friend. He was one of a hundred boys I went to school with at Saint Michael's."

"I wasn't going to—"

"Was there another wallet?" Dominic asked, looking at the back pocket of the victim's jeans. There was a worn outline from what a wallet would make but there was none.

"No," the officer answered. "Just that one."

"That's odd," Dominic said. "When did someone report this?"

"I told you, we received the call around ten this morning," Howard said.

"Who reported it?"

"According to the dispatcher, the neighbor. Uh—" Howard looked at the officer.

"Wayne Hodges."

"Where is he?"

"Outside?"

Howard nodded his head as if making a mental note. "Who are those people out front?"

"Beats me," the officer answered and shrugged his shoulders slightly, but Dominic noticed.

"Why don't you go find out if one of them is the neighbor."

"Should I bring him in here?"

"No. Just have him wait for me outside. I'll be out in a bit. Don't let anyone inside except the coroner. He should be here any minute," Howard said. Dominic heard the disgust in his tone.

"Yes, sir." The officer slipped past Dominic and out the front door.

"Did they find the gun?" Dominic asked.

"I don't think so," Howard said, looking around the kitchen. "But that's not unusual. What would be is if the killer left the weapon behind."

"True," Dominic agreed.

"What do you think happened?" Howard asked.

"Good question," Dominic said, looking at the room and the entry hall. "My guess would be Cody and Samuel were getting ready to eat dinner. Someone came in through the front door. Cody may have heard the intruder or seen him. Judging by the way the table looks and the broken wine bottle on the floor there was a struggle. Samuel may have made it out the door but by the time Cody tried, he was shot in the back."

Howard nodded as he looked around the room. "Sounds plausible. But, try this on for size. Cody was getting ready to eat dinner. Samuel came through the front door. Cody heard him and started to stand up. That's when Samuel shot him in the back. Cody fell against the table before falling to the floor. That sounds more like it."

"Then how did his wallet end up here?"

"Clumsy?"

"Hardly. I knew them both and Samuel would never harm Cody, much less shoot him."

"How do you know that?" Howard asked, eyeing Dominic suspiciously.

Dominic shook his head and kept silent.

"Well, either way, we have a killer on the loose and we need to find him," Howard said. He looked around the room again and then at the license in the wallet. "I don't get it. Why was Cody here? His family lives about two miles away."

Dominic shook his head. "I have no idea."

"What do you know about this Samuel Coffey?"

"Not much. I met him three months ago when I was working the switchboard. He and Cody came in. They wanted to see your old buddy, Brother Gregory."

Howard grimaced. "Oh, don't remind me of him. He never let me forget knocking him into the fish pond," he groaned. "Do you know why they wanted to see Brother

Gregory?"

Dominic shook his head. "No, I don't. While they waited for him, we chatted. Samuel seemed like a nice guy. Sort of reminded me of us, best friends who would do anything for the other."

Howard looked at the body again and frowned. "Well, not so much like us."

"So, now what?" Dominic asked.

"Let's take a look upstairs. I have a feeling one of them has been staying here for some time. Then we'll go find the neighbor, Mr. Hodges," Howard said, glancing at the body before heading toward the hallway.

There was a commotion at the front door. Dominic turned around to see. It was the coroner and his assistant.

"Come on, we'll give them room to work," Howard said. He walked into the hall and backed up against the bathroom door. Dominic followed.

The coroner, dressed in white, lightweight, hazmat coveralls approached Howard.

"Congratulations on your first homicide, Detective Miller."

"Yeah, this one's a little too close to home," Howard said.

The coroner raised an eyebrow.

"He's in there. Name's Cody Jacobson, twenty-eight," Howard continued.

"So young," the coroner said and shook his head. "Morning, Padre," he said to Dominic and continued into the kitchen.

"Come on," Howard said before Dominic had a chance to correct the coroner.

"Excuse me," the coroner's assistant said and scooted past them into the kitchen.

Dominic noticed the 35mm camera hanging from a strap around the assistant's neck. From his study, he knew it was standard procedure. Still, the thought of this being the last photograph of Cody tugged at his heart. He felt saddened for Cody's family and silently hoped they would never see the photos.

Howard was already starting up the stairs by the time Dominic reached the foot. He looked at the stacks of dust-covered books, magazines, and newspapers that leaned against the wall to the left. Carefully he followed on the right until he reached the small landing. The risers turned right with only four steps to the second floor. He continued up.

At the top of the stairs was a wide landing with two doors on the right and one on the left. A fourth door was to the left, beside the stairs. Dominic didn't have time to become curious as to where it led because Howard opened the door and announced, "Bathroom." Dominic watched and waited while Howard inspected the small room.

Walking back onto the landing, he said, "At least that room is clean. There are fresh towels on the rack and two toothbrushes in a cup by the sink. Even the floor has been mopped."

"Strange," Dominic said, remembering the state of the living room downstairs.

Howard walked toward the door at the back of the house, above the kitchen. It, too, had been cleaned. A four-poster bed looked freshly made with clean sheets. The nightstands on either side of the bed were dusted. The floor was swept and the windows were clear, free of a cloudy film of filth. Dominic noticed a book on the dresser, a Bible. He opened it and looked at the flyleaf. In neat cursive writing was the inscription

> *To my son, Cody,*
> *May you draw close to God through the*
> *pages of this Bible.*
>
> *All my love,*
> *Mom*

He closed the book and noticed the gold leaf on the edges of the pages had worn away from use. He smile faintly, happy with the thought Cody had heeded his mother's advice.

"Well, it appears that Cody was living here," Dominic said.

"That's what it looks like," Howard agreed. "Look what I found on the nightstand." He held up a small ring with several keys on it.

"What do you suppose they go to?

"Good question. My guess would be the front door and possibly that old truck outside," Howard said, examining the heads of the keys. "Someone obviously gave them to him," he said and brushed past Dominic.

Dominic put the Bible back on the dresser. He was about to follow him but something caught his eye. A small velvet box. He opened it and saw a man's ring.

"Coming, Charlie?" Howard called from the hallway.

Dominic quickly snapped the box closed and stuck it into the pocket of his habit. He hurried onto the landing. Across from what appeared to be Cody's room were two doors. Howard was standing at the door on the left. Dominic joined him.

The room was empty but the floor was swept clean and window sill dusted.

"Well, he certainly was tidy. I'll grant him that," Howard said and moved to the door on the right.

The room was just as neat and tidy as the other two, however, this room looked like a storage room. A single bed was against the outer wall on the right. Several boxes were stacked on top of it. On a small nightstand at the head of the bed was a brass candlestick holder with a candle that was half burned.

Howard walked over to inspect the boxes. He opened one and found a bunch of men's clothes. He dug deeper and found a Bible. He opened the cover.

"Looks like this stuff is Samuel's," he said.

Dominic had walked across the room and was staring

out the window. Howard joined him. The window faced the street but the leaves of the oak tree hid it from view.

"I would have loved a room like this when I lived with my grandparents," Dominic reminisced.

"Well, the view from our dorm was better than this," Howard said dismissively.

"True, but I bet whoever grew up in this room really liked it."

"Or they wished that stupid tree wasn't there," Howard said. "There's not much of a view of anything but the porch roof and that tree. Come on," Howard said.

Dominic took one last look out the window then turned around to follow Howard back to the landing and down to the first floor.

When they reached the foyer, the coroner and his assistant were carrying a stretcher out the front door. To Dominic's surprise, the stacks of newspapers against the wall were gone. Howard noticed it as well. He followed the coroner out onto the porch.

"What did you do with—" Howard spotted the missing newspapers piled in a heap on the front lawn. "What on earth?" he shouted.

The younger officer quickly went to him. "We had to move them for the coroner, sir," he said.

"You do realize there is a back door to the kitchen," Howard said.

"Yes, but...." the rookie officer looked over his shoulder as if for help from his partner.

Howard shook his head in disgust. "So, who are they?" Howard nodded toward the couple still standing across the street but now talking with a woman and another man with a camera.

"The woman is a reporter from the Silverton paper. The other two are the people who live in that house."

"What's she talking with them about?"

"I don't know. They don't know anything."

"So, you interviewed them?"

"No. My partner interviewed the guy who lives on the other side of the hedge."

"Why didn't one of you speak with them?" Howard asked, disgusted by the rookie's lack of following procedure.

The rookie just shrugged. "Do you want me to go do it now?"

"No, I'll do it myself," Howard said and headed for the street.

Dominic quickly followed.

When the reporter saw the two approaching she ended her interview with the couple but turned her attention to Howard. The couple slipped away, back to the front porch of their house.

"Diane," Howard greeted the reporter with a polite nod.

"Detective Miller," she responded formally, though Dominic could sense they knew each other and not just through work. "Can you tell me what happened here?"

"No comment," Howard said.

"Is it true you found a body?"

"No comment."

"We have witnesses who say a young man was murdered inside that house. Can you confirm that much?"

"You'll get the full story once we have all the facts," Howard said.

"What's a priest doing here?"

"Oh I'm—"

"Observing," Howard interrupted Dominic, holding his hand out as a gesture for Diane and her cameraman to leave. "Please. We'll talk later."

Diane took a step closer to Howard and put her hand on his cheek. "I'll hold you to that," she said as seductively as she dared in front of Dominic. Turning away, she said to her cameraman, "Come on."

Dominic watched the pair return to their van that was parked in the gravel driveway. He turned back to Howard.

"Before you say anything," Howard held up his hand. "We're not here to discuss my personal life."

"I didn't say anything," Dominic said.

"Good, keep it that way." Howard turned away and headed for the porch. Dominic followed. "Morning," Howard greeted the couple. He took out his badge and showed it to them. "I'm Detective Miller and this is Brother Dominic from the Abbey."

The couple appeared to be in their mid-fifties. The man wore a baseball cap. He was dressed in a blue work shirt and denim jeans and heavy boots. His boots were dusty, giving the impression he worked his farm. His wife was a wisp of a woman, thin, tanned, with her greying auburn hair pulled back in a loose bun on the back of her head. She wore a simple knee-length house dress with flat-soled, cloth shoes.

"Nice to meet you, Detective. I'm William VanDyke and this is my wife Claire. What can we do for you?" the man said, holding out his hand to Howard for a quick handshake. He nodded at Dominic.

"I'd like to ask you a couple questions if I may?" Howard said.

"Sure," William said with a bit of indifference in his tone.

"What can you tell me about the man who lived across the street?"

"The homosexual?" the man said.

Dominic's eyes widened and he shook his head at the man. Luckily Howard was standing in front of him so he didn't see, but the householder did.

"What makes you think he was gay?"

"Oh, I just assumed," William said. "I mean, when I saw the other young man moving in, I just..."

"So, there were two men living there?"

"At least that is what it looked like to me."

"What else can you tell me about them?" Howard said. Dominic detected a bit of annoyance in his friend's tone but not that anyone who didn't know him would notice.

"I only met the first guy, Cody, I think that was his name. He was nice, always very friendly and polite. The other one I never met. I just saw him moving boxes into the house yesterday morning."

"Samuel," Claire said.

"Samuel?" Howard repeated.

"Yes. I went over to say hi to them and took them a plate of cookies."

"I see." Howard scribbled in his notebook. "So, who owns the house?"

"Good question," William said. "The owner passed away a couple years ago and the house has sat empty ever since. Well, until Cody moved. Wayne Hodges, he's the neighbor next door, he's been keeping an eye on the place. I've seen him lurking around the outside, peeking into the windows."

"Interesting," Howard said.

"Yeah. He tends to act like he owns everything on that side of the road. Ever since Mr. Whitaker passed away, it's as if Hodges has taken over ownership of Whitaker's house and land."

"Weren't there any heirs?"

"None that ever came around since we've lived here. We bought this place nearly…" he glanced at his wife.

"Right after we were married," she said.

"Twenty years ago." William said. "Whitaker could have had grown children, but we never saw them."

"How long ago did you say Mr. Whitaker pass away?"

"Oh," again, William deferred to his wife.

"It was four years ago last June. The house sat empty for a little over three years before Cody moved in," she said.

"When was that?" Howard asked

"It was right after Thanksgiving last year," Claire said.

"Did you happen to see or hear anything last night?"

"Well," William said, removing his baseball cap and

scratching his head. Dominic's suspicions were correct. Mr. VanDyke had a crewcut but he was also balding on top. William put his cap back on. "It's pretty quiet around here most of the time. So, any unusual noises do catch one's attention." He glanced at his wife who nodded at him. "Around midnight, I was awakened by someone screaming but it stopped before I had a chance to see who or what it was about. I looked out of our bedroom window." He turned and gestured toward the window on the second floor of his farmhouse. "But it was too dark to see anything. I thought it was odd because usually Hodges burns his outdoor lights all night. He even installed one on a pole and aimed it at Whitaker's house. Said it was for security purposes. But for some reason it was off last night."

"Could you tell if the screaming was a man's voice or a woman's?" Howard asked.

"To tell you the truth, I was sound asleep and the scream woke me. I wasn't sure it wasn't part of a dream," William said. "I still don't know."

Howard nodded.

"Detective, can you tell us who was killed? We saw the coroner carrying someone out."

"I'm sorry. We need to notify the family before we can be sure."

"I see," William said with a nod. "It's an awful shame. I don't envy you or your job."

"Thanks," Howard said and smiled. "We'll leave you but I may have more questions later."

"Sure, glad to be of help if I can," William said.

Howard and Dominic headed back across the road to the other neighbor's house.

"I still can't understand why anyone would kill Cody," Dominic said as they walked up the gravel driveway that separated the hedge from the neighbor's two-story house.

"When we find who did this, we'll know why," Howard said.

Dominic took in the view of the neighbors' property. It was obvious that they took pride in their home. The large front lawn was well watered and freshly mown. The flower beds would rival Brother Fiacre's beautiful flower beds at the abbey.

The screen door opened as the pair walked up the front porch steps. A rather portly, elderly man wearing denim jeans with suspenders and a plaid flannel shirt with patched elbows on the sleeves stepped out onto the porch. The expression on his face told Dominic he wasn't pleased to see them.

"Good morning," Howard said as he approached the man. He withdrew his badge from his pocket and held it up. "I'm Detective Miller, and you are…?"

"Wayne Hodges," the man answered. His voice was rough and gravelly but his tone seemed relaxed.

"I was told you phoned in about what happened next door?" Howard put away his badge.

"Yeah, yeah," he answered as he shook his head from side to side. "Sad, sad." He looked past Howard at Dominic. His expression changed from a sympathetic expression to a scowl. "What's a priest got to do with the police?"

"Oh, I'm not a priest. I'm just one of the brothers at—"

"This is Brother Dominic from Saint Michael's. He's accompanying me today," Howard explained, interrupting him.

"Well, I don't need no religion," the man scoffed, then dismissively pawed the air and turned his head away.

"We're not here for that," Howard said. "I'm here to ask you a few questions about the young man who lived next door."

"Squatted, you mean." The hostility in Wayne's voice caught both Dominic and Howard by surprise.

"Uh, yes, I guess," Howard said, trying to recover and get control. "May we go inside and have a word?" Howard asked.

"Why?"

"I just thought you might be more comfortable sitting down while we talked."

Wayne looked at Dominic again and then back at Howard. "I suppose," he said and opened the screen door.

"Thank you," Howard said and entered.

Dominic could tell Mr. Hodges didn't care for him, so he simply nodded as he passed in front of the man and entered the house.

Howard stopped in the cozy foyer and looked around at the striped papered walls and the antique framed photographs of presumably family members from the past.

"Do you live alone?" Howard asked as Mr. Hodges joined them.

"No, but now it's now just the Mrs. and me. The kids have all grown up and moved on. This way." He herded them into the living room to the left of the foyer.

"You have a lovely home," Howard said upon entering.

Dominic looked around the room. He agreed, it was a nice home. In some ways it reminded him of his grandmother's house and now her apartment. Pressed doilies covered the armrests on the sofa that sat against the inside wall facing the large front window that had a view of the front lawn, road, and a corner of the VanDyke's house. Two matching leather swivel rocking chairs were placed beneath the window and faced the sofa. A coffee table with a couple magazines and a copy of the newspaper sat in the center of the room between the sofa and chairs. At the end of the living room, opposite the foyer was a red-brick fireplace. Knick-knacks decorated the mantle.

"Suppose you want to know what I heard?" he said, gesturing for them to have a seat on the couch while he sat down in the chair closest to the fireplace. "I already told that young cop."

"Yes, he told me you did, but I need to hear it directly from you. Sometimes secondhand isn't as accurate," Howard explained. He pulled out a small notebook from the inside breast pocket of his suitcoat. From another pocket, he took out a pen. "Now, first of all, do you know who owns the house next door?"

"Of course I do, Tom and Erma Whitaker. They lived there for years. After Erma passed, Tom stayed in the house for a couple more years before he followed her."

"Who owns the house now?"

"Good question."

"Did they have any children?"

"Oh, they had a couple boys as I recall. One is gone. The other I think lives in Arizona. He showed up for the funeral but went back. He wouldn't even step foot in the house. I've been keeping an eye on the place ever since."

"How long has that been?"

"Four or five years," Wayne answered as if it didn't really matter. "No one's supposed to be living in there. The power's been shut off."

"Well, it appears that someone has been and from the looks of it for quite a while."

"Yeah, I know," Wayne said.

"Do you have any idea who?"

"Nope." Wayne shook his head.

"What about Mrs. Hodges? Would she know?" Dominic asked.

"No!" he answered sharply.

Dominic glanced at Howard.

"Can I ask her?"

"No. She's not here. She went to town to get her hair done. She goes every week on Saturday morning."

"But this is Monday," Howard said.

"Well, she missed her appointment last week."

"I see," Howard said, glancing at Dominic. "From what we could tell, at least one young man was living there and there are no signs of forced entry. We also found a set of keys. So, someone must have given them to them. Do you know who has the keys?"

Wayne's lips tightened. He looked away toward the hearth. "I'm the only one with the keys and I can assure you, I didn't give them any. Maybe they picked the lock?"

"That's possible," Howard agreed but Dominic could tell he didn't buy it.

"Can you walk me through what happened?"

"Sure. The Mrs. and I watched the evening news and then Dallas. The Mrs. likes that actor who plays JR. Me, I'm not much for that sort of show but she likes for me to watch it with her."

"Okay, then what?"

"Well, after Dallas was over, the Mrs. and I were about to turn in for the night when we heard a truck pull in next door."

"Did you see the truck?"

"Yeah, caught a glimpse of it just before it turned into the driveway. A beat up old red Ford."

"Is it the one that is still in the driveway?"

"Yep."

"Did you see another car?"

"Nope, just the pickup. That's probably why I didn't know anyone was squatting there."

"But if you saw the truck, surely you knew someone was there," Dominic said.

Wayne glared at him. "The truck belonged to Mr. Whitaker."

"I see," Dominic said, but another question popped into his mind. He decided not to ask.

"So when you saw someone was driving it," Howard said. "Didn't you question it? Go see who it was?"

"No."

"Why not?"

"How the hell should I know? I just didn't."

Howard nodded and wrote in his notepad. "So, what happened after the truck pulled in?"

"I went to bed," Wayne answered.

"Did anything else happen?"

"Well, as I lay there beside the Mrs.," he said, looking directly at Dominic. Dominic didn't react. His living a celibate life was not a problem for him, but it was obvious Mr. Hodges took exception to it. He continued, "We heard some yelling and then it was quiet for a moment. That's when we heard the truck backfire and speed off."

"The truck? Are you sure?" Howard asked.

"Well, at the time I thought it was the same truck."

"I see," Howard said, and scribbled another note. "I'm sorry, go on."

"Well, that's pretty much it. After the truck left, everything was quiet again. So, we went back to sleep."

Howard nodded and then tilted his head slightly to the side. "When did you realize what had happened?"

"Not 'til around ten this morning. I peeked my head around the hedge in back and saw the backdoor was open so I went to see what was going on. That's when I found the body."

"I see," Howard nodded. "Do you own any guns, Mr. Hodges?"

"Practically everyone around here does. You don't think I—I don't like what you're insinuating. I think you better leave." Mr. Hodges stood up.

Howard rose to his feet. Dominic quickly followed his cue. "One more question before we go. Why didn't you burn your outside lights last night?"

"I'm not answering anymore questions. Get out!"

Dominic watched the old man's eyes and made mental note of how he reacted to the question, especially how he clenched his fists.

"Okay," Howard said calmly. "We'll be going but I may need to speak with you again."

"You can speak to my attorney," Mr. Hodges said while he ushered them toward the front door.

Dominic followed Howard out onto the front porch and then down the driveway to the end of the hedge.

"He was a bit defensive," Dominic said, glancing back at the house. Mr. Hodges was gone.

"Yeah, reminds me of the old saying, the one who screams the loudest is the one hardest hit."

"What? I've never heard that before. Where did you come up with that?" Dominic said

"I don't know, I picked it up somewhere, but it's true."

Dominic laughed and shook his head.

"Did you notice how he goaded you? At first I thought he had a problem with you, or with religious people in general."

"I noticed," Dominic agreed.

"The man has issues."

Howard headed between his car and the squad car for the front steps where the other two officers were standing and talking with each other.

"Good, you're still here," he said. "I think we're done here for now. Go ahead and secure the scene. Here," he tossed them the ring of keys he found. "Lock the doors and seal them. Then tape off the doors and windows for good measure."

"Roger, that," the officer said.

"Take the keys to the station and bag them for evidence. Put it on my desk. Do you have that?"

"Yes, sir."

Dominic turned his attention away from watching Howard to the pickup. He squatted down by the rear tire on the driver's side to get a closer look at it. Just as he thought, the sidewall had been jabbed with something sharp. He stood up.

"What are you doing?" Howard asked. "You're a little old to be playing hide and seek."

"I was looking at the tires. Look, this one was purposely flattened."

Howard squatted down for a closer look. He stuck the tip of his pen into the slit and examined the cut. Standing up he said, "Let's check out the passenger side."

They walked back around the bed of the truck. The tire on the passenger side had the same puncture mark.

"I'd say it was intentional."

Dominic walked around the truck to the driver's door and glanced inside. Dust covered the seat and dashboard. "Howard, come see this."

Howard joined Dominic and they peered through the window.

"No one has driven this truck in a long time," Dominic said.

"Which means, Mr. Hodges was either lying or he saw a different truck," Howard said. "Stay here, I want to check something."

Before he could respond, Howard headed across the road to the VanDyke's house. Left alone, Dominic decided to have a look around the back of the house.

The gravel driveway led to an old barn that looked as though it would collapse at any second. There were large gaps between the wall boards that let sunlight through. It did not look safe at all.

When he turned away from the barn, he noticed a new telephone pole at the end of the hedge that separated Hodges' property from the Whitaker's. A large floodlight was mounted to the top of the pole and aimed at the back of the house. Dominic shook his head and continued on his way.

The backyard was a patch of tall weeds. An old, weathered, wooden umbrella-shaped clothesline stood in the center of the yard, away from the shade from the trees. The rusted remains of a free-standing, bench swing made Dominic think of the one his grandparents had on Tam O'Shanter Drive.

The sound of someone approaching startled Dominic

and he turned around. "Oh, it's you," he said, seeing the officer Howard gave the keys to.

"Hi, Father."

"Oh, I'm not a priest. It's Brother, Brother Dominic."

"What's the difference?" the officer asked.

"A priest is ordained and can issue the Sacraments. A brother is someone who has taken vows."

"Oh, like a male nun," the officer said with a bit of a smirk.

Dominic grimaced. "Yeah, like a nun," he said.

He followed the officer to the back door and watched as he closed and locked it. The officer then took a large sticker from his back pocket and peeled off the backing. He applied the sticker to the edge where the door met the doorpost. Dominic realized if anyone were to open the door, the seal would tear and the officers would know their crime scene was compromised.

"Find any more clues?" Dominic asked.

The officer looked at him. "Shouldn't you be with Detective Miller?"

"He went across the road to the neighbor's."

"Well, we're about done here, so you might want to wait in his car."

"Good idea," Dominic said. He turned away and headed back to the front of the house.

Howard was returning from across the street and they met beside his car.

"So, what did you need to talk to them about?" Dominic asked.

"I wanted to ask them about the truck and if they heard another one."

"And…"

Howard glanced back across the road. "They said the truck hasn't moved from that spot in years. So, Hodges is lying."

"Or he's mistaken."

Howard looked at Dominic and frowned. "He's hiding something."

"Did they say if they heard anything?"

"No. Only someone screaming." Howard shook his head and reached for the door handle. "Come on, we need to see if we can find this Samuel guy. If he's not the shooter, then he's a witness and he could be in serious danger." Howard took the wallet from the plastic bag and opened it. He pulled out the driver's license and read the address. "Eastview Lane, Silverton. That's not too far from here." He put the license back into the wallet and set the bag on the front seat between them.

CHAPTER THREE

Howard pulled the car away from the curb and headed south on Meridian. Dominic knew where they were going. According to Samuel's drivers' license, the last address he lived at was about two miles away.

Dominic stared out the window while he struggled with his obedience to the Abbot and his loyalty to his friend. *But Samuel was my friend, too,* he silently reasoned. *There is no way he is capable of murdering anyone, and especially not Cody.* Dominic decided to heed Abbot Ambrose's order to keep silent about Samuel. He would go along with Howard for now.

Howard turned onto Eastview Lane. The farmland turned into forests of oak and fir trees on both sides of the road. The only evidence of homes were the rural mailboxes on wooden posts at the pavement's edge. Howard slowed so he could read the numbers on the boxes.

"There it is," he said and stopped the car on the shoulder of the road. He checked the license one more time to be sure. Satisfied they had arrived, he turned up the gravel driveway.

The two-story house was not visible from the street. It

was well-kept, with yellow exterior walls, white trim, and white ornamental shutters. The lawn was well watered and green. A rusty swing set stood at the far edge of the lawn away from the driveway. The driveway widened to allow parking for at least three vehicles, but there was only one, an old, burgundy, Oldsmobile Cutlass.

Howard parked the car beside it and stared at the house for a moment. "I wonder if he lived here alone?"

"There's only one way to find out," Dominic said.

"I suppose so."

Howard exited the car first. Dominic quickly followed and joined him at the front bumper. Together they made their way to the front door. Howard stepped forward and rang the bell.

The sound of footsteps could be heard before the door opened. A young girl about nine years old with bright red hair stared up at them.

"Hi," she said with a grin.

"Good morning, is your mom or dad home?" Howard asked.

"Yes, I'll go get them." She closed the door and left them standing on the front steps.

Dominic chuckled. "She's cute." But he quickly regained his composure when the door opened again.

A tall, slender woman with greying red hair and blue eyes, smiled at them. "Yes?"

"Good morning, ma'am. My name is Detective Miller and this is Brother Dominic from Saint Michael's Abbey." He showed her his badge. The smile vanished from the woman's lips. "Is this the Coffey residence?" Howard asked.

"Yes. I'm Sarah Coffey," she answered.

"Do you know a young man named Samuel?"

"He's my son," she answered. Dominic noticed her smile fade to a look of worry, concern, and fear.

"May we come in?"

"S-sure," she answered hesitantly, stepping back and

opening the door wider so they could enter. "Go get your father," she told her daughter who immediately ran deeper into the house.

Dominic entered the small foyer and looked at the living room to his left. A floral sofa sat beneath the front window. It appeared a bit worn but its upholstery was still holding up. The same couldn't be said for the olive green, vinyl recliner sitting across from the sofa. A hole in the footrest exposed some of the padding, and the fabric on the armrests was dirty from years of use.

Sarah led the way into the living room and quickly scooped up the scattered pages of a newspaper and a few stray toys before inviting them to sit.

"That's okay," Howard said, trying to stop her from tidying up.

She put the paper and toys down on the coffee table.

"Is your husband here?" he asked.

"He's out back in the garage. I sent Jane to get him," she answered. "Would you care for some coffee?"

"As tempting as that sounds, I think we should wait for your husband."

Sarah bit her lower lip. "What's this about? Has something happened to Sam?" she asked, wringing her hands in an effort to stop them from shaking.

"I—"

The sound of her husband's heavy footfalls interrupted Howard. A moment later, from the back of the house a burly man with short salt-and-pepper colored hair, heavy five o'clock shadow, and a square jaw entered the room. He was still wiping his hands with an oil-stained rag. He looked Howard and Dominic over.

"What's this about?" His tone was gruff.

"Mr. Coffey, my name is Detective Miller and this is Brother Dominic from Saint—"

"I don't care where," Coffey interrupted. "What do you want? We aren't buying anything or joining your church."

"No, we're not here for that," Howard said. "Please, would you both have a seat?"

Sarah sat down. She looked at her husband. Her eyes filled with tears. She held out her hand to him. He walked across the room to her but remained standing.

"I'm not in the habit of repeating myself, Detective. What is this about?"

"We're here about your son, Samuel."

"He doesn't live here anymore," Mr. Coffey said dismissively. "I threw his ass out of here a month ago. Pardon my French," he paused and then pointedly said, "Padre." A smirk on his face.

"It's Brother," Dominic said, noting the man's sarcasm.

Mr. Coffey shrugged, showing his indifference.

"Please, Mr. Coffey," Howard said, gesturing for him to sit beside his wife on the sofa.

Mr. Coffey clenched his teeth and glared at them. Slowly his hostility melted away when he saw the seriousness in their eyes. He sat down.

"We're trying to find Samuel. We have reason to believe he may be hurt or in danger."

"What? Why?" Mr. Coffey asked.

"He may have witnessed a murder last night."

"A murder?" Sarah gasped and covered her mouth with her hand.

"Yes," Howard said with a nod.

"What makes you think he was there?" Mr. Coffey demanded, his voice full of disbelief.

"We found his wallet at the scene."

Dominic watched as Mr. Coffey's expression change from skepticism to shocked realization.

"You don't think he's in danger. No. You think he did it! I'm not saying anything more. You can leave now."

"No, we don't—" Dominic said.

"I said, get out!" Mr. Coffey's voice thundered throughout the house. Howard took a step back.

"Okay, but if you change your mind—"

"We won't," Coffey said and began to usher them toward the front door.

"We really don't think he killed anyone," Dominic said as they returned to the foyer. "But whoever did may have seen him and could be after him."

"Nice tactic, Padre," Mr. Coffey said. "I'm not buying it. Go and don't come back."

"If we do come back, I assure you we'll bring a warrant," Howard said as they returned to the front porch.

"You do that."

The door slammed shut.

When Howard and Dominic reached the car and opened the doors, a young woman stepped out of the shadows of the trees.

"You cops?" she asked.

Dominic, startled, turned around and faced the young woman. She was thin, almost too much so, which made the floral dress she wore hang on her like on a clothes hanger. Even with her black sweater with sleeves that covered most of her hands, she looked as though a strong breeze would knock her over. Her long, brown hair hung down past her shoulders. She folded her arms over her stomach.

"Is it that obvious?" Howard asked.

"Not really. It's just I know all their friends and you aren't one of them. And since you have this nice car, you wouldn't be interested in buying one of their old junkers. So, what's going on?" she asked.

"And you are?" Howard asked.

"Carolyn Hathaway," she answered. "I suppose you're here because of my brother Sam."

Howard closed his door and walked to the tail end of his car. "As a matter of fact, we are."

"It's about time. Did he finally report that bastard?"

Both Howard and Dominic exchanged surprised glances.

"Report who?" Howard said.

"Our stepfather, Leroy Coffey"

"Wait a minute. I'm confused. So, Mr. Coffey isn't Samuel's father?"

"Oh hell no. Our dad died when Sam was still a baby. I was five. Mom married that ass-hole and changed our last names."

"So, I'm guessing you changed your name back to your father's?" Dominic asked.

"Not legally, but I've been using Hathaway for the last nine years."

"I see," Howard said, nodding his head.

"I don't think you do," Carolyn said and started to back away.

"Wait!" Howard called out.

"Why?"

"If you see your brother, could you let him know we're looking for him?"

Carolyn eyed them both suspiciously. "Why are you looking for him."

"He may have witnessed a murder last night."

Carolyn took a step closer. "A murder? Who?"

"I can't say just yet."

"Cody?" she said, looking at Howard and then at Dominic as her expression turned grievous. "Oh God. Oh God." She started backing away into the shadows

"Don't go," Dominic said, but she turned away and ran into the woods. He started after her but stopped at the tree line and turned back. "She's gone."

"Come on, Charlie," Howard said. "We should go."

Back in the car, Dominic sat staring straight ahead. "She knew Cody."

"Of course she did," Howard said as he started the engine.

"No, I think there was more. I think she may have been in love Cody."

"I'm not saying it couldn't be." Howard said and pulled the car back onto the main road. "But she is nearly four years older than Cody."

"So? Don't you date older women?"

"Really? You're making this about me?"

"I'm just saying it's not unheard of, is it?"

"Maybe," Howard said, shrugging his shoulders slightly. "How would I know."

CHAPTER FOUR

"So, where to next?" Dominic asked as they headed toward town.

"We need to tell Cody's family. After that, I think we could use a drink."

Dominic's eyebrow raised and he smirked. He glanced out the window as Howard drove past the Whitaker farmhouse.

"What do you think about what Miss Hathaway said about them renting the house?" he asked.

"I think we'll need to talk to Mr. Hodges again. I wonder what else he's lied about."

They continued north until reaching E Marquam Rd NE. Turning left, Howard drove west. He picked up the mic on his radio and asked for a confirmation of the Jacobson's address.

"Ten four," he said and returned the mic to the clip on the side of the radio. "We're almost there. Any thoughts about what to say to them? I mean, how do you tell someone their son's been murdered?"

"Haven't you done this before?"

"No, this is the first time," Howard admitted.

"Well, I wouldn't lead with the word murdered. Remember your training, and be empathetic."

"Empa-what?"

"Put yourself in their shoes, but be kind and gentle. It's going to be a shock no matter what you say but…"

"Okay."

Howard turned onto Kaiser Lane and headed northeast. At the end of the first hop fields, he slowed and turned into a gravel driveway. At its end stood a two-story house surrounded by a green lawn and bookended by two, large leaf maple trees.

Dominic followed Howard to the front door and watched him knock.

A woman answered. She was wearing a bibbed apron pinned to her white blouse and tied about her waist over her ankle-length dark blue skirt. Her dyed brown hair was pulled back and twisted into a bun on the crown of her head. Dominic noticed the dye had stained her scalp at the hairline. She looked at them and smiled.

"Hello, Brother Dominic," she greeted and opened the screen door. "Who's your friend?"

"Hello, Mrs. Jacobson. This is Detective Miller from the police."

She looked at him and her eyes lit up. "Howard Miller?" she gasped. "Oh my, you've grown into such a handsome man. If I were thirty years younger…" she winked at him and blushed. "Oh my, what can I do for you? What brings you out here?"

"Is Mr. Jacobson home?" Howard asked.

"He's out with Craig in the back fields helping with the harvest."

"Is there any way to get in touch with him?"

"We have a CB radio. I could call him. Is it important?"

"I'm afraid so," Howard said.

Mrs. Jacobson looked at Dominic who nodded. Her cheery expression was overshadowed by one of concern and worry. "Won't you come in," she said and held the door for them.

Once they were inside, she led them into the kitchen at the back of the house. "Go ahead and have a seat at the table," she said, continuing to the wooden desk by the backdoor. A CB radio sat on a shelf above the desk. She picked up the mic and called her husband.

"John, can you come home right away?"

"What is it Margaret?"

"Detective Miller and Brother Dominic from the Abbey are here. They need to speak to us."

"I'll be there at lunch, can't it wait?"

"No, John. Now," she answered firmly.

"This better be good, Margaret. I'm on my way."

"Ten four, base out," she said and put the mic down. Turning around she looked at the two. "Suppose you heard?"

"Yes, ma'am," Howard said.

"He's very busy, harvesttime. He's up at dawn and doesn't come in until sundown."

"I understand. I wouldn't bother him but it is very important," Howard said.

"While we're waiting for John, can I get you something cold to drink? Lemonade? Soda?"

"Lemonade sounds wonderful," Dominic said and started to stand up.

She gestured for him to sit. He obeyed.

The kitchen table reminded Dominic of the table in his grandmother's kitchen. He ate his meals and did his schooling there when he was a young boy, before he was sent to the abbey.

"I hate this," Howard whispered.

"I know," Dominic responded.

"Here we go," Margaret said and set a tall glass of lemonade in front of each of them. She sat down across from Howard and took a sip from her glass.

Dominic and Howard followed suit.

"Oh my," Dominic said. "This is the best lemonade I've had in a long time."

"John likes the freshly squeezed instead of the frozen or powdered stuff you get at the grocery store. It takes quite a few lemons but it's worth it."

"I'll say," Howard agreed.

"Too bad Cody isn't here. I'm sure he'd love to see you both. He moved to Portland several months ago. He got a job at the telephone company there."

"Oh, really?"

"Yes," Margaret said. It was obvious she was proud of her son. "I'm so happy he has an office job. Now he doesn't have to work out in the weather like his father."

Dominic looked at Howard. Feelings of guilt stirred from deep in his gut. He wished they could leave, but he knew they couldn't. He reminded himself it was better they find out about Cody from them instead of a stranger or reading about it in the newspaper.

Another fifteen minutes passed before the back door opened and John walked into the kitchen. The stereotypical farmer in bib overalls, sweat stained and dusty white t-shirt, and heavy boots. He took off his baseball cap to reveal his crewcut white hair that made his face look ruddy. He walked over to the sink and helped himself to a glass of water before turning around and looking at his guests.

"What's the meaning of this?" he said, impatiently. "I don't have time for a visit. I've got a crop to get in."

"I'm sorry, Mr. Jacobson. Please come and have a seat," Howard said.

"This is my house! I don't—"

"John, please," Margaret said and pulled out the fourth chair.

"Fine, but make it quick." He walk across the kitchen to the table and sat down.

"When was the last time you saw Cody?"

John turned to his wife and shrugged his shoulders

slightly. "I don't know, maybe ten months, a year?"

"It was Thanksgiving of last year. Just before he moved to Portland," Margaret said.

"How did he seem to you?"

"Fine. What's this all about? Why the sudden interest in Cody?" John demanded.

"I'm afraid I have some bad news," Howard said. "Cody didn't move to Portland."

"That's nonsense," John said. "He calls us every weekend. Why just yesterday, after Mass, he phoned. He even said he met someone and thinks he's in love."

"I don't know anything about the calls but I know for a fact, he's been lying to you."

"How dare you call me out of the fields to sit in my own house and defame my son. I think it's time you both leave," John said and started to stand up.

Margaret, who had been staring at Dominic, grabbed his arm. "John, please." He sat back down. "Please, tell me what's happened," she said.

"This morning I received a call," Howard said. "Someone had found a body in an abandoned house just east of town." He paused and looked at them. "It was Cody. Cody is dead."

Margaret gasped and clutched her chest with her right hand and grabbed John's hand with her left as tears instantly filled her eyes.

John bolted to his feet, nearly knocking over the half-full glasses of lemonade on the table. "Is this some sort of a sick joke?" John shouted. "First you accuse him of lying to us and now you tell us he's dead? No! You're the ones who are lying. I want you to leave."

Howard stood up. Dominic followed his cue.

"I'm sorry, it's true, Mr. and Mrs. Jacobson," Dominic said.

"But he moved to Portland," Margaret said while tears streamed down her cheeks.

Dominic shook his head.

"Oh, God," Margaret whimpered. "John." She reached for him.

John stood motionless, his mouth agape and his eyes staring blindly at the table. When Margaret's words finally registered in his ears, he looked at her and dropped back into the seat beside her. She wrapped her arms around him and sobbed.

"No!" she nearly screamed in his ear. "My baby!"

Dominic's vision became blurred as tears filled his eyes. His throat felt as if someone were gripping it. "I'm so sorry." His voice was a whisper. He withdrew a handkerchief from the pocket in his cassock and dried his eyes. Glancing at Howard he noticed he too was touched by their grief and pain.

John looked at Howard. His eyes red and damp. "I don't understand. How?"

"We don't have all the details, yet," Howard said quietly. Dominic could hear the strain in his voice. "What I can tell you is he had been living in an abandoned farmhouse since right after Thanksgiving."

"But his job…" Margaret's voice was weak.

"I don't know," Howard said, matching her tone. He looked at John. "He was living there with a young man named Samuel Coffey. Do you know him?"

John's lips tightened into a thin, angry line. "Yes," he said as if the word left a bitter taste in his mouth. "He came around the summer before last looking for a job, so I gave him one. He didn't last the season. He showed up late and was always complaining about one ache or pain or another, especially the day after payday. I think he was a drinker and brawler. There were several times he came in with a black eye. I warned Cody to stay clear of him."

"Do you think he had anything to do with…" Margaret couldn't finish her thought.

"No," Dominic said, causing Howard to look at him.

"Actually, we're not sure. We're still looking for him. He may have witnessed what happened and could be in danger," Howard said.

"Oh dear," Margaret murmured, shaking her head.

"What happened to him?" John asked.

"Do you know if he had a gun?" Howard asked.

"No," John answered, confidently. "He hated guns. I tried to teach him how to shoot but he would have none of it. Why? Was that—"

"I'm sorry to have to tell you but, yes, Cody was shot."

John's head jerked back. "Oh, God."

"He didn't feel it. He died instantly," Howard said.

Dominic looked at him in shock. He quickly looked away and turned to the Jacobsons. "Is there anything I can do for you? Do you need anything?"

"No," John said. He looked at Howard. "Just find the son of a bitch that did this to our boy and make sure he pays for it."

Margaret continued to weep.

"Are you going to be all right?" Dominic asked.

"I don't know," she answered. "Can you pray with us?"

"Sure," Dominic said.

They recited the Lord's Prayer and a Hail Mary, before Dominic asked God to watch over the Jacobsons. When they concluded their prayer, Howard stood.

"Well, that will be all for now," he said. "We do need at least one of you to come down to the coroner's office to make a positive identification."

"When?" John asked.

"Either later today or first thing in the morning. I'll let you know."

Dominic rose to his feet. Margaret stood as well.

"I'm so sorry," he said and gave her a hug. She wrapped her arms around him and quietly cried into his chest. When they parted, she looked at them both.

"I'm thankful it was you two who brought us the news,"

she said.

Howard stepped forward and gave her a quick hug and a gentle kiss on her cheek. He turned to John and held out his hand but John stepped forward and wrapped his arms around him in a bear hug.

"I'm sorry," he told Howard before releasing him.

"Think nothing of it," Howard assured him. "We best be going."

"I'll check back with you later. Make sure you're okay. You'll both be in my prayers," Dominic told Margaret.

"Thank you. Cody always spoke well of you," she said and followed them to the front door.

"If you think of anything that might be helpful, please call me," Howard said, handing John a business card.

"I can't imagine what that would be," he said. He handed the card to his wife.

Once outside, with the Jacobsons out of earshot, Dominic turned to Howard. "Why did you tell them that about Cody?"

"What?"

"That he died instantly?"

"I don't know. I just thought if they thought he didn't suffer, it would be easier on them," Howard said. "Besides, you can't be telling them that Samuel isn't a suspect. We don't know that."

"But we do," Dominic said.

"How do we know?"

"Cody wouldn't have asked him to move in if he didn't trust Samuel."

Howard stared across the top of the car at Dominic while he thought about it. "I suppose so," he said and opened the driver's door.

Once they were both buckled in in the front seat, Howard put the key in the ignition and started the car.

"Samuel is not off the suspect list yet. We need to find him, first. For all we know he could be dead as well."

Dominic stared at Howard. He struggled again with the urge to tell him Samuel was safe and back at the Abbey. "Okay," he said as Howard backed the car off the driveway onto the street.

As they started toward town, Howard radioed the office and told them he was back.

"What's next?" Dominic asked.

"We need to find that gun. Then we'll find the person responsible," Howard answered. "But first, I need something to eat and drink. How about you? You hungry? It's on the department."

"Sure," Dominic answered.

"I know a place that we can have some privacy to talk and that has great food. I took a date there last week," Howard said.

Dominic's eyebrow raised and the corners of his mouth curled slightly. "Was this the gal from last night?"

"Nah. She wasn't the dinner type."

"Dinner type?" Dominic asked, raising an eyebrow.

"She was more of a bar date."

"I see," Dominic said, but really didn't know the difference.

"Don't get me wrong. She has the looks, just not the deep conversational type."

Dominic stifled a laugh. If there was one thing Howard wasn't, it was deep. Lost in memories of the hours they spent studying for Howard's police exams, Dominic realized he hadn't heard a word of what Howard was saying.

"That only takes you so far, trust me." Howard laughed. "Oh, I took a new gal, Rachel, out last Friday. She was not my usual type at all. Brunette, a bit—oh, how can I make it sound polite?"

"Just say it," Dominic said, sounding a bit bored. He had heard all about the women Howard had dated over the years and at this point he had lost count. Sometimes he wondered if Howard could get serious with anyone.

"She's a bit of a nerd."

Dominic's head pulled back, and he looked confused. "What do you mean?"

"All she talked about was computers and how they will be the next great industrial revolution."

"Really? I bet that was a short date."

"No, we had a great time."

"So, are you going to see her again?"

"Probably. She's out of town for the next two weeks. Her job sent her to Seattle."

"Seattle's not all that far."

"True. But now I have this case to solve. I need to keep focused."

Howard pulled into a parking spot in front of Edelweiss Steak Haus.

Dominic looked at the building, with its traditional German façade complete with shutters and flowerboxes. He liked the warm, homey feeling it gave him. He opened his door and stepped out of the car. The midday air was warm but there was still a bit of a nip of the coming fall in it.

"It looks like we've missed the lunch rush," Howard said, joining him on the sidewalk. "Good, we can talk without being overheard."

They entered the restaurant and were quickly shown a table in a back corner, away from the windows. The waitress, dressed in Bavarian attire with a white blouse with short puffy sleeves, knee-length black skirt and white apron, handed them each a menu before leaving to get their glasses of water.

"Remember, this is on me, or should I say, the town."

"Are you sure? I do have money," Dominic said.

"I know, but yes, I'm sure."

"Well, the Schwenkbraten sandwich looks tasty. I think I'll have that with potato salad."

"Don't tell me, tell the waitress," Howard teased. "I think I'll have the cheesesteak sandwich with sweet potato fries."

They both closed their menus when the waitress returned.

"You ready to order?" she asked.

"Yes," Howard spoke first.

After taking their order, the waitress left. She returned with two tall glasses of cola.

"Would love a beer but I'm on duty," Howard told Dominic. Beer was something Dominic never acquired a taste for. It was just bitter water. Howard enjoyed it though, a little too much at times. They took a sip of their colas.

"This is my first big case since becoming a detective," Howard said. "I can't mess this up but I'm worried."

"Why? Because of our connection to Cody?"

"No," Howard answered. "Because, I can't figure out the motive? I mean, we have the neighbor across the street who seems to be on the up and up. And then the other who claims he's supposed to be watching the house but says he didn't know anything about Cody living in the house, but is really renting it out on the Q.T.

"Then we have the Jacobsons. They're a good Catholic family. Seemingly no motive to harm their son. But, Mr. Jacobson obviously didn't think much of Samuel."

"I was thinking about what he said, how after paydays Samuel showed up with bruises and complaining about pain."

"Yeah, I noticed that, too. I think we will be talking with Mr. Coffey again. And speaking of them, what a mixed up, messed up family."

"It's called dysfunctional, nowadays," Dominic interjected.

"Well, if you're looking for a motive Mr. Coffey has a good one. Cody leaving threatened his livelihood."

"But would he kill over it?"

"People have killed for less," Howard said. "Once we get the coroner's report, we'll have a better understanding about what happened. Meanwhile, do you think you can find out what Cody and Samuel saw Brother Gregory about?"

"Sure," Dominic answered with a nod.

"Good," Howard said, glancing toward the kitchen. "Where's our food? I'm starved."

"You sound like Gus," Dominic said.

"I'm serious," Howard said. "I didn't get breakfast this morning."

Dominic laughed.

"Say, speaking of Gus, have you heard from him, lately?"

"I received a letter from him last week. I still have to answer him," Dominic said, making a mental note to write him soon. "He's loving his job. He's excited because the company is working on a new home computer. I honestly don't understand the whole concept, but he does."

"Oh, not computers again," Howard groaned. "Does he have any girlfriends?"

"None that he's told me about," Dominic said and sipped his cola. "I think his job is his focus."

Howard shook his head. "I had such hopes for that kid."

"He's still young. There's time for him to settle down. But, you, on the other hand…"

Howard stopped and put his drink down. "And what's that supposed to mean?"

"Oh, nothing," Dominic teased and laughed.

The waitress returned and set their plates on the table in front of them.

The rest of their lunch break they spent eating their meal in near silence. Occasionally Howard would moan in an imitation of ecstasy while he ate his sandwich, a sound that reminded Dominic of their friend Gus and caused him to laugh quietly to himself. Other than that there was only a smattering of small talk until they finished their meal.

Back in the car, Howard started the engine. "I'll take you back to the Abbey. The coroner won't have anything for us until later today or even tomorrow. Meanwhile, you can talk with Brother Gregory. Find out what Cody and Samuel had to say. I'll pick you up tomorrow morning after Mass."

Dominic nodded. "Okay."

CHAPTER FIVE

When Dominic arrived at the abbey he stopped at the reception desk just past the lobby doors of the monastery wing. He smiled at Brother Jonah, his former high school nemesis, Dougary Duggan. The monastic life had really changed him and they were now like brothers.

"Hey, Jonah, any messages for me?"

"Yes," Brother Jonah answered and pulled a slip of paper from one of the hundred and forty message boxes on the wall behind the crescent shaped front desk. He looked at the message and handed it to Dominic. "Abbot Ambrose wants to see you in his office when you return."

"Thank you," Dominic said with a smile. "I guess I should go now." He turned around and returned to the lobby. Across the hall were the doors to the students wing. Dominic took a deep breath and crossed the room.

"Ave," Abbot Ambrose called in answer to the knock on his door.

Dominic entered but stood holding the door open. "You wanted to see me?"

"Yes," Abbot Ambrose said and put the letter he was reading down onto his desk. "Come in and close the door, please." He stood up and walked the short distance to the seating area.

Dominic closed the door and then joined his superior. He waited for the Abbot to sit before he sat in the chair next to him. The chairs were turned slightly toward each other to make conversation easier.

"What did Howard want to see you about?"

"There was a murder last night just east of town."

"Why would that involve you?"

"The person who was murdered was Cody Jacobson."

Abbot Ambrose's expression saddened and he leaned further back in his chair. "Oh, no."

"He was living in an old farmhouse that sat abandoned for years. What's more, Samuel had just moved in with him."

Abbot Ambrose looked away for a moment. "You mean, Samuel could be the—"

"No, I don't think he did it. I think he saw who did, though and that means he could be in danger."

"I see."

"Has Samuel said anything?"

"No. He is still in shock."

"Can I see him? Maybe he'll talk to me."

"Don't get your hopes up. Sometimes it takes days, weeks or even years for a person to recover after experiencing a trauma."

Dominic nodded that he understood, but he had to try to reach him.

"Was there anything else?" Abbot Ambrose asked.

"Howard is considering Samuel a suspect."

"You didn't tell him about Samuel, did you?"

"No. I didn't. I don't believe Samuel did it. I want to see if I can find out who did before Howard makes matters worse."

"Good. Take whatever time you need. Father Anthony will continue to cover your classes."

"Thank you, Abbot Ambrose. May I be excused. I really want to see Samuel."

"Yes, son, go. May God bless you in your efforts."

Dominic left the office and headed to the infirmary on the third floor of the monastery wing. In the years after joining the monastery, the infirmary had moved from its former location and now had a view of the cloister garden behind the abbey building. It was a better view than it had before. Brother James thought it would be more healing for his patients.

The infirmary a large room, much like the dorms of the seminary high school. Ten beds lined the interior wall so that everyone who wanted could look out the windows across the room. On either side of each bed was a curtain suspended from the ceiling. It could be opened to allow the occupants to speak with each other or closed for privacy. Right inside the infirmary's entrance was a small reception desk where Brother James' assistant Sister Mary Francis sat. She was a registered nurse and the only woman allowed past the front desk downstairs. She looked up as Dominic entered.

"Good afternoon, Brother Dominic," she greeted him with a warm smile.

"I was wondering if I could look in on Samuel," he whispered.

"Brother James is with him," she said, nodding into the room. Dominic glanced down the row of beds. The curtains were closed around the fifth bed. "But I'm sure it would be okay."

"Thank you, Sister," Dominic said and quietly walked past the other beds, three of which were occupied by napping individuals.

When he reached Samuel's bed, he paused and watched as Brother James finished taking Samuel's blood pressure.

"You're doing just fine," he said to his patient, but received no response. Brother James glanced over his shoulder and noticed Dominic. "Ah, come to see our patient."

"Yes," Dominic said. He noticed that Samuel was now dressed in a hospital gown and had been cleaned up.

"There's been no change, I'm afraid."

Dominic looked at Samuel. The head of the bed had been raised so he was sitting upright. He continued to stare blindly across the room.

"He hasn't said anything?" Dominic asked.

"Not a word."

"Is it okay if I just talk to him?"

Brother James looked at his patient. "It couldn't hurt." He slipped past Dominic and returned to his office behind the reception desk.

Dominic took a chair from the corner and brought it beside Samuel's bed. He sat down facing the young man. Samuel's right hand was resting beside him on top of the blanket. Dominic put his hand over Samuel's and watched, hoping for a response but there was none.

"Hello Sam. You've been through quite an ordeal. You're safe here," Dominic said softly. "I know you were moving in with Cody." Still no reaction. "Were you and he close?" Nothing.

Dominic spent an hour talking to Samuel about nothing and everything that came into his head, hoping that something would spark a reaction, but nothing did. Finally, tired, Dominic rose to his feet, his hand still resting on Samuel's. When he started to move it, he felt Samuel's hand twitch, and he froze. Sitting back down he put Samuel's hand in his while he stared into Samuel's distant eyes.

"Do you want me to stay?" he asked. "Squeeze my hand if you do."

Samuel's hand moved slightly, then his fingers curled around Dominic's hand. Still his eyes were unchanged. Dominic patted the top of Samuel's hand.

"Okay, Sam, I'll stay," he said. "I met your sister this morning. She's worried about you. She doesn't know where you are and I didn't tell her. I could bring her here if you want to see her." Dominic waited for a reaction but there was none. Even the slight grip lessened. "Sam, please come back to us. Tell us what happened, what you saw."

Samuel didn't move. He continued to look at nothing but his eyes began to tear.

"Did Carolyn know Cody? Did she like him?"

Nothing.

"She has strong feelings about your step-father. She doesn't like him at all."

Nothing.

"Do you know Mr. Hodges? He's the neighbor on the other side of the hedge."

Nothing.

"Mr. and Mrs. VanDyke seem nice."

Samuel's hand twitched.

"Do you like them?" Dominic asked and stared at Samuel's hand. He noticed another twitch but he didn't know what it meant.

Brother James walked up behind Dominic. "How are you two getting along?"

Dominic stood up and released Samuel's hand. "There were a couple moments when I thought he might come out of whatever this is, but…"

"Give him time. His mind is probably still trying to process whatever it is that happened. But, it's almost time for Vespers, and I think he could do with some rest."

"Okay," Dominic said. He turned back to Samuel. "I'll stop by and see you later." With that, Dominic returned to the hallway. He still needed to speak with Brother Gregory but it would have to wait until after Vespers and dinner.

After dinner, Dominic went to see Brother Gregory. He

found him sitting on a bench at the edge of one of the ponds in the Great Lawn.

"Good evening, Brother Gregory," he greeted the elderly monk.

Gregory looked up and squinted his eyes. "Dominic?"

"Yes, Brother."

"These old eyes aren't what they used to be. Sit," he said and scooted over a bit. "How are you?"

"I'm doing all right," Dominic said. "How are you?"

"Oh, as good as any eighty-nine year old is, I guess. Can't complain too much."

"Well, you haven't changed a bit," Dominic said, though in truth he had. In the last few months, Brother Gregory had lost weight though he didn't have any extra to lose. It made his black habit hung on him and appear two sizes too big. His cheeks were sunken. He was beginning to look positively skeletal, like the pictures of the Grim Reaper in a library book Dominic had checked out when he was a student.

"What brings you outside? I don't usually see you out."

"I was actually looking for you."

"Me? Why so?"

"I was wondering if you could help me with something. I've noticed Cody Jacobson and his friend Samuel have been visiting you a lot."

Brother Gregory nodded. "Yes. Fine lads."

"Would you mind telling me your impression of their friendship?"

The old monk cocked his head and looked at Dominic. "I don't know what you mean?"

"Well, did they appear close?"

"They seemed like good friends."

"Do you think they would ever harm one another?"

Brother Gregory eyed Dominic suspiciously. "What aren't you telling me?"

Dominic hesitated and looked down at the fishpond.

The sun was slipping below the horizon, casting a bright pink, red, and blue reflection in the shimmering water. He turned back to the senior monk. "This morning, Detective Miller—"

"Miller? Miller? Howard Miller?"

"Yes, Brother Gregory. He's working for the local police and is a detective now. Anyway, there was a murder last night in an old farmhouse east of town." He paused, looking for any reaction. There was none. "It was Cody, Brother. Cody Jacobson was killed."

Brother Gregory crossed himself and bowed his head for a second. He turned and looked at Dominic. "I see," he said. "And you are wondering if his friend could have done it?"

"I'm not," Dominic said. "But Howard does. But he doesn't know Samuel." He reached into his pocket and pulled out the small ring box. Carefully he opened it and showed the contents to Brother Gregory.

"Nice ring. Where'd you get it?"

"I found this on Cody's dresser. Did he ever mention anything to you about this?"

Brother Gregory shook his head but kept staring at the ring. "No. Not that I recall."

Dominic closed the box and put it back in his pocket.

"You probably shouldn't have taken that from the scene."

"I know, but I couldn't let Howard see it."

"Why?"

"Because if what the neighbors suspect is true, Cody and Samuel could be homosexuals."

"Bah!" Brother Gregory scoffed. "There's no way either of them could be."

"Really? Why?"

"Because I can tell, that's why. You don't spend sixty-nine years in this business without being able to read people."

"I see," Dominic said. He felt his shoulders relax but he didn't know why. "But, you're sure neither one of them would harm the other?"

"I suppose there's always the possibility but not with those two. They were the best of friends. You tell that *Detective* Miller he's barking up the wrong tree, as usual."

Dominic had to stifle another laugh. He stood up. "Thank you, Brother Gregory. Do you want to head back inside before it gets too dark?"

"Sure," he answered and reached out, grabbing Dominic's forearm as he rose to his feet. He picked up his cane with his other hand.

The two made their way back to the abbey.

After taking Brother Gregory to his cell, Dominic returned to his room. He pulled out a fresh composition book and began to write himself notes about what he had found out and what questions still remained on his mind. By the time he was finished, it was time for bed.

CHAPTER SIX

The next morning, after Mass, Dominic went to the kitchen. When he opened the door, he was struck by the aroma of freshly baked bread. The cooks, three nuns from the convent in town, were placing the hot loaf pans on the cooling racks of a tall bakery cart. One sister noticed him and she nudged the taller one beside her. She glanced at Dominic and a smile spread across her lips.

"Charlie," she said. "Give me a minute."

Dominic nodded and pulled a stool from beneath the huge wooden table that sat in the center of the kitchen. Sitting down he watched quietly while they finished. He took the composition book from the pocket in his habit and opened it. As he reviewed his notes, he couldn't help feeling as if he had missed something.

"Well, Charlie, what a surprise," Sister Faith said. She kissed his cheek and set a couple coffee mugs down on the table in front of him. The kiss startled him out of his thoughts.

He quickly closed his notebook and looked at his mother. It was hard for him to believe she had actually joined the convent where she had been hiding out for most of his life. With his uncle, her brother, securely in jail for his crimes, she was free to come out of hiding but instead of returning to the world, she joined the Sisters of Saint Benedict.

"I thought you were supposed to be in class?"

"I'm helping Howard with a police matter."

"Oh? Does he know you're down here?" she asked as she sat down on a stool beside him. She reached out and took the coffee pot from the center of the table and poured them each a cup.

"I left word where I am with reception. They'll send him here."

"I see," Sister Faith said, cocking her head slightly and eyeing her son. "What's the matter? Don't you want to help him?"

"I do, really, but I'm not sure I am."

"Why do you say that?"

"It's a murder investigation. Howard seems positive that this one particular guy did it, but I don't think so. I think Howard may be rushing to conclusions because this is his first real case since becoming a detective."

"I see. Is there anything else bothering you?"

"I have this feeling that I've missed something, something important."

"Have you talked about this with Howard?"

"I tried yesterday."

"Well, if you feel that strongly about it, talk to him again today. You have a good head on your shoulders and good instincts. He'll listen."

"I hope so."

Sister Faith put her hand on his and gave it a squeeze. "Now, have you visited your grandmother lately?"

"Not since last Sunday. Why? Is she okay?"

Sister Faith smiled. "Yes, she's fine. She's been spending a lot of time with another resident, a Mr. Sinclair."

"Oh yes. I've met him. He's very nice. At least I think

so. Nothing's wrong with that is there?"

"No," Faith laughed. "She seems to be very happy is all."

"I'll have to go see her once we solve this case."

"You do that," Faith said, glancing at the doorway behind Dominic. "I think someone is here for you."

Dominic turned around in time to see Howard enter the kitchen.

"Good morning, Sister Faith," he said as he approached the table. "Do you have another cup of coffee?"

"Of course," she said and stood up. "Black isn't it?"

"Yes, please."

"Why don't you two go into the staff dining room. I'll bring it to you there."

"Thank you," Dominic said.

The two headed for the small room behind the kitchen sinks. In the center of the room was a dining room table that seated six. A portrait of the newly elected pope hung on one wall while a painting of Mary holding the baby Jesus on her knee hung on the opposite. A window on the south wall gave a view of the baseball field.

Dominic pulled a chair out and sat down. Howard took a seat at the end of the table beside him.

"How was your morning?" Dominic asked.

"Not great. The captain wanted to see me, wanted to know how the investigation is going."

"But it's only been twenty-four hours?"

"I know, and as he so eloquently reminded me, *the first twenty-four are the most critical.*"

"So, any other news?"

"Here you go," Sister Faith said as she entered the room and interrupted them. She set a cup of hot coffee in front of Howard along with a small pot and plate of pastries. "There are plates and napkins in the sideboard."

"Thank you," Howard said. "I didn't mean for you to go to any trouble."

"It's no trouble at all. If you need anything more, just let one of us know."

"Thank you, Mom," Dominic said as Sister Faith left the room.

"That is so weird," Howard said, shaking his head. "Sort of creepy, even."

"What?" Dominic looked at him with his eyebrows pinched above his nose.

"You calling a nun, Mom."

"But she is."

"I know, but it's still weird." Howard let out a laugh and picked up an apple fritter with a thick coating of white sugary glaze. Dominic quickly grabbed a plate and some napkins before Howard set it down on the table.

"So, as I was saying, any new developments?" Dominic asked and sat back down.

"I received the coroner's report. The victim—"

"Cody," Dominic interrupted.

Howard frowned at him. "We're supposed to keep it impersonal, otherwise we can't do our job and remain objective."

Dominic nodded. He understood but he still didn't like the thought that Cody was just another generic person, a nameless statistic.

Howard continued. "As we already know, the victim was shot in the back. A single bullet just below his left shoulder blade. The bullet struck his heart and he died within a matter of a couple minutes."

Dominic made the sign of the cross and shook his head.

"Mr. and Mrs. Jacobson are coming at eleven to make a positive ID. I'd like you to be there. I have a couple questions I forgot to ask them. Then I'd like to go back to the house to have another look around," Howard said, taking a huge bite of fritter and a sip of coffee.

"That sounds like a good idea. I can't help but feel that I've missed something. I'd like to take another look myself."

Howard cocked his head and looked at Dominic. A grin spread across his face. "Look at you."

"What?"

"You know, you should be a detective and not a high school English teacher."

"Oh, knock it off."

"Look, if it weren't for you I wouldn't have passed my exams. You studied just as hard as I did all through my months at the academy."

"You did it on your own."

"That's not true and you know it. You as good as audited all of my classes. I bet if you took the exams, you'd pass with flying colors. Just imagine, Detective Miller and Detective Brother Dominic."

"Don't be silly. Abbot Ambrose would never approve of such a thing, and even if he would, I'm not sure I'd want to. Now, focus. Back to the case at hand."

After eating a fresh maple bar and wrapping a cinnamon twist in a paper napkin for later, Howard thanked Sister Faith and the two left.

Howard drove his car down the two lane road from the Abbey into downtown. The coroner's office was located next door to the hospital in Silverton. In the rural setting, traffic was never an issue. They arrived with thirty minutes to spare.

John and Margaret Jacobsen arrived right on time. John fiddled nervously with his baseball cap in his hands. Margaret kept dabbing her eyes with a white handkerchief she took from her purse. They greeted Howard and Dominic when they entered the waiting room.

"The coroner will be out in a moment," Howard said. "He will then lead you to where they have the body."

"You'll come with us, won't you?" Margaret asked, looking at Dominic.

Dominic glanced at Howard who nodded. "Yes," he said to them. "We both will."

At ten after eleven a door opened and a man in a white lab coat walked into the waiting room. He was a portly little man with a round face, heavy black-rimmed glasses, and a bald head which reminded Dominic of the turtle mascot from a wax commercial.

"Mr. and Mrs. Jacobson," he said, though it sounded like a question.

"Yes, that's us," John said, his voice strained.

"We'll be coming with them," Howard informed the coroner.

"Very well. Please follow me."

The coroner led them down a narrow hall to a large glass window. He instructed them to stand in front of it while he went inside the room. A body lay on a stainless steel gurney and draped with a large white sheet.

Dominic had already seen Cody's body at the farmhouse, but standing there, looking through the window at the gurney felt different. When the coroner removed the sheet over Cody's head he saw Cody's face, Dominic couldn't breathe for a moment. It was a shock, even though he looked so peaceful, as though he were just sleeping.

Margaret burst into tears and put her hand on the glass window while she covered her mouth with the hanky in her other hand. John nodded to the coroner as tears rolled silently down his cheeks.

The coroner replaced the sheet and returned to the hall.

"Thank you, and I'm so sorry," he said.

The four returned to the lobby where they sat down. The coroner joined them with some papers for them to sign. Howard waited for them to regain their composure before he spoke.

"Yesterday, you told me that Cody moved to Portland."

"Yes," John answered.

"Did Cody own a car or truck?"

"He had a small red pickup," Margaret said.

"A Ford Ranger," John added. "It was a bit beat up

from using it on the farm. But it ran well enough. Why?"

"Nothing specific, just curious." Howard started to turn away but stopped. "You don't happen to know where it is do you?"

John gave him an annoyed look. "How the hell should I know. My son is lying dead in the other room."

"Mr. and Mrs. Jacobson, may I have a word with you in my office?" the coroner interrupted.

"I'm sorry," Howard said. He motioned with his head for Dominic to follow him outside.

"I'm so sorry," Dominic said. He gave Margaret a brief hug and shook John's hand before following Howard out to the car.

"Well, that went horribly sideways," Dominic said when he reached the car. "What was that about?"

"Last night it dawned on me, how did Cody get his stuff to the house? He must have had a vehicle, but we didn't see one at the house. I wonder if Samuel took it. I'll check the DMV records and find out the license plate number and put out a BOLO for it."

Dominic didn't say a word. He opened the car door and sat down in the passenger seat.

"I want to take another look at the house before we go check with the neighbors again. Find out why Hodges is lying about renting the house."

CHAPTER SEVEN

In no time Howard and Dominic arrived back at the farmhouse. Mr. VanDyke, the neighbor across the street, was out in front of his house watering his lawn with a garden hose. He waved to them. Dominic politely waved back.

Howard parked the car behind the old pickup. Stepping out of the car, he eyed the yellow police ribbon that was strung around the vehicle and house warning curious snoopers to keep away. It didn't look disturbed which was a good sign.

Turning around, he said to Dominic, "Let's go have a word with Mr. VanDyke." The pair walked across the street.

William, seeing them approaching, shut the water off. "Good morning," he greeted them.

"Good morning," Howard said.

"You're back?"

"Yes, I wanted to let you know that we can now confirm that it was Mr. Jacobson who passed away. He was shot."

William nodded. The corners of his mouth turned down. "So horrible. He was such a kind man. To have that happen...I can't imagine."

"Well, we have some more checking to do." Howard said and started to turn away, but stopped and turned back. "Say, do you recall seeing another truck across the street, a red Ford Ranger?"

"Now that I think about it, yes. But it was usually parked toward the back of the house."

"Did you happen to see it the day before yesterday?"

Mr. VanDyke's brow furrowed and his eyes squinted. "I can't say for sure—no, yes. Now that you mention is, that was the day that other fellow moved in. They were in the red truck."

"I see. Well, thank you," Howard said.

"I have a question," Dominic said, stopping Howard from leaving. "Do you know who slashed the tires on the old pickup?"

"Slashed the tires?" William repeated, looking surprised and a little confused. "No. You might have to ask Hodges there. He might know."

"Okay. Thank you. Have a good day," Dominic said. He followed Howard back to the road.

"Nice one," Howard said. "I completely forgot about the tires."

When they reached the farmhouse, Howard raised the crime scene tape so Dominic could pass beneath it. Then he followed.

"I want to try to walk through the scene," Howard said while he unlocked and opened the front door.

"The shooter had to come through the front door in order to sneak up on the victim while he sat at the table with his back toward the entryway. Since he didn't turn around, he must have known his assailant. That would mean Samuel."

"That makes no sense," Dominic said. "If the assailant snuck up on Cody, it wouldn't matter if he knew him or not. He wouldn't have heard him. Say it was Samuel and Cody heard him, he still would have turned around to greet him."

"Okay, true. But I'm still leaning toward Samuel. Hear me out. Assuming the front door was locked at the time since it appears they weren't supposed to live on the first floor, it couldn't have been anyone else." Howard said as he looked at the living room.

"That's a lot to assume," Dominic said. "What if the person had a key?"

"Then the victim would have heard it and at least turned around to see who it was."

"Not necessarily. I mean, if you were going to kill someone, you'd be as quiet as possible, wouldn't you?"

"Sure."

"So, the assailant could have made it inside without being heard. But he doesn't know about the creaking floorboards and steps wrong. Cody hears, turns, sees the gun, jumps to his feet to run and…So, there's the possibility of someone other than Samuel being the killer."

"A slim possibility," Howard said, as he stopped outside the kitchen door. "Now, we know from the position of the body, the shooter was in the hallway here. That would mean the victim was seated at the table with his back to the doorway. Based on the amount of food and plates on the table, it was a dinner for two. So, Samuel must not have sat down yet because the other chair was still pushed up to the table. That means he could have come up behind his victim and—"

"Sounds like you've already made up your mind and are just trying to build a case."

Howard looked at Dominic with a puzzled expression. "What's the matter with you? Why are you protesting so much? What aren't you telling me?"

"Nothing. From what I know of Samuel and Cody's friendship, neither would or could have harmed the other, let alone killed them. And even Brother Gregory agrees."

"Oh, so, based on your feelings and those of an old man, we should ignore Samuel as a suspect?"

"Howard," Dominic said shaking his head out of frustration. "What's the motive?"

Howard pursed his lips and took a deep breath, letting it out slowly through his nose. He did not look happy with his best friend at that moment.

"Fine, then you tell me."

"We have Mr. Hodges next door. He's secretly renting the house to Cody. Perhaps he feels Cody letting Samuel move in was threatening his little side business?

"Or what about Mr. VanDyke across the street? I noticed the look on his face when he said Cody and Samuel were homosexuals. I don't think he's as openminded as he wants us to believe.

"And then there's Samuel's stepfather. Samuel moving out means he's lost a big chunk of income.

"So, there are three other good possibilities right there."

Howard's face relaxed. He took another breath before he spoke. "Four, but I'll withhold judgement until we have more facts."

"Okay," Dominic said. He felt a bit of relief that Howard seemed willing to consider an alternative. "So, now what?"

"Let's walk through each scenario," Howard said. "So, according to the coroner's report, the killer was between ten to twelve feet from the victim when he fired." Howard walked into the kitchen and starting at the table, paced off ten steps and turned back around to face the kitchen. "He would have fired from about here at the foot of the stairs."

"Sounds reasonable," Dominic said. "Then what?"

"The truck out back. Let's take a look."

Dominic followed Howard through the kitchen and out the back door. Ducking under the yellow tape, they stood in the backyard.

"Did anyone check the barn?" Howard asked.

"I don't know. I didn't," Dominic answered.

Without a word, Howard started for the old, dilapidated

barn. Carefully he started to slide open the large main door.

"Hey, you! Get away from there. Leave that alone," a man's voice shouted.

Howard stopped and looked past Dominic. Dominic turned around to see Mr. Hodges standing by the end of the hedge.

"Just what do you think you are doing?" he said and started for Howard.

Howard held up his badge. "I'm Detective Miller."

"I know who you are," Hodges shot back. "What are you doing with that barn?"

"I'm beginning to search it."

"There's nothing in there."

"Why don't you let me be the judge of that."

"Unless you have a search warrant, I think you should leave."

"May I remind you, this is not your property," Howard said. "And this is a murder investigation."

"I-I—" Mr. Hodges stammered. "Fine! If you get yourselves killed, don't say I didn't warn you." He turned around and left in a huff.

Dominic joined Howard at the barn door. They both watched until Mr. Hodges was out of sight.

"Wow! That was odd," Howard said.

"Sounds like someone is hiding something," Dominic said.

"True," Howard agreed and turned back toward the door. "Let's have a look."

"Be careful," Dominic warned.

Slowly Howard slid the door open, letting the late morning sunlight shine inside. He coughed and cleared his throat. The dust covering everything inside was thick.

Dominic looked at the ground and noticed what appeared to be fresh footprints.

"Have a look at this," he told Howard.

They both took a closer look.

"Barefoot," Howard said. "Who would come out here barefoot?"

"Beats me, but there must have been a reason." Dominic looked around without moving. The barn was about the same size as the house. It wasn't for animals, though. A long, built-in workbench spanned the side wall to the left. A large tractor sat in back, partially covered by a canvas tarp.

"Here," Howard said.

Dominic took a couple steps into the barn and looked to where Howard was pointing.

"Tire tracks," Howard said. "They must have parked the pickup in here. But where is it now?"

"And how and when did whomever take it?" Dominic said.

Howard walked deeper into the barn. "Those footprints lead clear back here." He stopped beside the tarp before continuing to the back of the barn behind the tractor.

Dominic hesitated, looking up at the beams and underside of the roof, deciding on whether or not it was safe to venture further. Not completely confident the barn wasn't about to collapse, he joined Howard.

Behind the tractor was an open door to the outside. They both went to take a look. The tall dry grass appeared to have been trampled. Whomever made the footprints left through this door.

"Curious," Howard said. "Let's go have a word with old man Hodges."

The pair walked back through the barn and closed the large door, leaving it as they had found it. Dominic followed Howard across the driveway to the next-door neighbor's house. They walked up the front steps and knocked.

When the door opened, a short, stout woman with grey hair pulled back in a bun greeted them with a warm smile. To Dominic, she reminded him of the actress who played Aunt Em in *The Wizard of Oz*. He smiled back at her.

"Yes?" she said, looking through the screen door.

"Good morning, you must be Mrs. Hodges?"

"Yes, I'm Martha Hodges," she answered. "I'm afraid I'm not buying anything today."

"Oh, we're not selling anything," Dominic said.

"I'm Detective Miller," he said, holding up his badge. "and this is Brother Dominic from Saint Michael's Abbey. We're looking for your husband. Is he around?"

"I'm sorry, you just missed him. He left a few minutes ago. Said something about needing to go to Silverton or Salem. I can't recall. I was busy with the breakfast dishes when he left. Is there something I can help you with?"

Howard glanced at Dominic. "Sure."

"Please come in." Martha opened the screen door and held it for them.

"Would you care for some coffee, I just made a fresh pot?" she offered.

"Coffee would be nice," Howard said and watched Martha leave the room.

"Wha—"

"It makes them feel relaxed when you accept their offer," Howard said. "Then they will talk more."

Dominic nodded.

Martha returned to the living room with a tray and three steaming cups of coffee, a cream pitcher and a bowl of sugar. "I wasn't sure if you put anything in your coffee," she said as she set the tray down on the low table in front of the sofa.

"Black is fine for me," Dominic said. "Thank you."

Howard picked up his cup and took a sip. "Oh my, that is a wonderful cup of coffee."

"Thank you," Martha said and smiled.

"I suppose you heard about the young man who was killed next door?" Howard said, taking another sip.

"Oh my, yes," Martha said. "That poor boy. Such a nice young man, I don't understand who could do such a thing."

"So you knew Cody?" Dominic asked.

"Yes," she said. "We used to have mid-morning coffee together every day."

"So you knew he was squatting in the house?"

"Oh, no. He wasn't squatting, my husband was renting it to him."

"Renting?"

"Yes, he thought it would help him keep an eye on the place since it's sat empty for so long."

"I see," Howard said. "Tell me, did you hear anything or see anything two nights ago?"

Martha shook her head. "No, but then our bedroom is upstairs and faces the back. We couldn't see or hear a thing."

"So you wouldn't know if anyone drove up next door?" Howard asked.

"Not unless we were out front. The hedge between us and the Whitaker house is much too overgrown for us to see."

"Makes sense," Howard said with a nod.

"Mrs. Hodges, does your husband own any guns?" Dominic asked.

"Yes," she answered. "Why?"

"Just curious. Seems as though everyone around here has them," Dominic said.

"Well, he has an old revolver that belonged to his father. He uses it to kill gophers and snakes out in the fields. He also has his hunting rifle but I don't know what it is. I really don't care much for guns. I've asked him to keep them out back in the barn."

"I understand," Howard said. "May I take a look? I like to hunt and see what other people use."

"Sure, I don't see why not," Martha said and stood up from her chair. "I'll get the key."

Dominic watched her leave the room. He couldn't believe how cooperative she was being. She didn't seem to be uncomfortable with any of the questions.

A moment later she returned, key in hand, and with a

smile on her lips. Dominic and Howard stood.

"Right this way," she said and led them through the kitchen and out the back door.

The back lawn was as well tended as the front with a flower bed filled with mums, and asters in bloom around its edge. In opposite corners of the lawn were tall oak trees. Beyond the lawn about a dirt path led to a two-story barn approximately fifty yards from the house.

"I'm sorry about the dust, Brother," she said.

Dominic looked down at the hem of his long habit. It was starting to turn grey with the fine dust. He shook it and some of the dust fell away. "Don't worry about it, Mrs. Hodges. It comes off."

"Here we go," she said and shooed away a few chickens who were pecking the ground in front of the side barn door. She unlocked the padlock and opened the door. Stepping inside, she flipped on the light switch and the room came into view.

It was a small office, with a desk and low bookcases. In the corner stood a tall black safe.

"Wayne keeps his guns locked in the safe," she said and led the way. She bent down slightly and began spinning the wheel on the lock, first to the right, then to the left, and finally back to the right. She spun the dial so quickly, Dominic couldn't make out the combination. She turned the metal handle and the door clicked open.

"May I," Howard said before she could open the door any farther.

"Oh, yes, of course," she said, taking a step back.

Howard opened the door wide, giving Dominic a chance to see as well.

Inside the safe was a double barreled shotgun propped in the back corner. A gun belt with bullets hung from a hook on the right interior wall of the safe. The holster was empty.

"Is this where your husband keeps his pistol?" Howard asked Martha.

"Why yes," she said with a puzzled expression. "I don't understand where it could have gone. Wayne is very meticulous about keeping it there unless he's using it."

"Would he have used it last night?"

"For what?" Martha asked looking at Dominic.

"After what happened next door, maybe he wanted the added protection in the house?"

"No. He knows I don't allow guns in the house. He would never bring it inside. He always keeps it out here."

"Well, thank you, Mrs. Hodges," Howard said and closed the safe. He gave the dial a spin. "Shall we go back to the house?"

As the three made their way along the narrow path, Howard continued to question Martha. "Do you remember when the last time Mr. Hodges had his pistol?"

"Oh, I'm not sure," she answered. "It could have been last summer, around the start. We had a gopher issue in one of the pastures. I don't recall him actually firing it, though."

"I see," Howard said.

"I have a question about the other night," Dominic said. "Did you happen to hear any gunshots?"

"Oh, yes. Woke me from a sound sleep. I turned over and Wayne wasn't there. It frightened me something awful, but then he came running up the stairs. He said he was just in the bathroom and heard the noise." She paused for a moment. "That's odd, we have a bathroom upstairs, and he had his slippers and jacket on over his pajamas." She shook her head as if shaking herself out of her thoughts. "I think he'll be back shortly."

"Well, thank you for the coffee," Howard said when they reached the backdoor. "We'll have to catch him another time. I'm afraid we must be going,"

"Thank you, Mrs. Hodges. You have been very helpful and very kind," Dominic said.

"I'm glad I could help," she said. "I'll let Wayne know you were looking for him."

Dominic stopped before he reached the corner of the house and turned back. "One more question," he said, taking a step back toward Mrs. Hodges. "It's sort of strange. Is Mr. Hodges right or left handed."

"Left," Martha said. "Is something wrong?"

"No, just curious," Dominic said. "I'm a lefty, too. Thank you. We'll see you later."

Howard and Dominic rounded the corner of the house and crossed the driveway to the hedge. Once they were back on the Whitaker side, Howard turned to Dominic.

"What do you make of that?" he asked.

"She sure has a different version of events than her husband. I lean toward her version because it makes more sense. Just looking at the house from the front, there is no way Mr. Hodges could have seen a truck arrive unless he was downstairs in their living room."

"Plus, she admitted that he was renting the house out." Howard said.

"What about the pistol? Do you think we should get a search warrant?"

"No. Chances are that's why he's gone to Salem…to pawn it. We'll never find it if he has. What was all that about being left or right handed?"

"Come on, I'll show you," Dominic said and headed for the back door of the Whitaker house.

Howard followed him into the kitchen and then into the front hallway.

"Now," Dominic said, holding up his left hand with his thumb raised and his index finger pointing outward. "Cody was shot in the back. If Cody jumped to his feet, a left handed shooter could still strike their target. Whereas, a right handed shooter would have to take a step left…" Dominic did and was halted by the staircase. He looked at Howard who stood with his mouth agape. "So, we now know our shooter was a lefty."

"You are amazing," Howard said. "I would never have

thought about that. Very good. See, you should be a detective."

"No, I like teaching," Dominic said. "It suits me just fine."

Howard shook his head. "What a waste. Come on, let's go see if we can find Miss Hathaway."

"Why her?" Dominic asked.

"I think we'll get straighter answers from her than her mother and step-father," Howard replied.

"What about talking with the VanDykes? Aren't we going to talk to them again?"

Howard glanced across the street. He smiled and waved at William who was still watering his lawn by hand. William raised his right hand and waved back.

"No need," Howard said, opening his car door. "He's right handed."

Dominic glanced over his shoulder at William. The neighbor waved again. Dominic waved back and sat down in the passenger seat. "Okay. I get it."

CHAPTER EIGHT

Howard turned the car south on Meridian and headed toward Silverton.

"How are we going to find her?" Dominic asked.

"I'm hoping she'll be at the Coffey's."

"Are you going to stop and ask them?"

"No," Howard scoffed and cast a disbelieving look at Dominic before watching the road ahead. "I'm just going to drive by and see if she's lurking in the woods."

"Oh, I see," Dominic said sounding suspicious.

"What?"

"What do you want to ask her about?"

"About whether or not her stepfather is left or right handed. You know, your idea."

"And…?"

"If she knows—" Howard glanced at Dominic who sat beside him with a grin. "Oh, knock it off. What are we, two again?"

Dominic laughed. Howard joined him.

"Seriously, I want to make sure she's okay. I got to thinking about her last night and how upset she looked before she took off."

"Yes, I was concerned about that as well," Dominic admitted.

When they neared the Coffey property, Howard slowed the Town Car to a near crawl. Dominic looked through the windshield at the forest. The sun was directly overhead which made it hard to see into the trees.

"Nothing," Howard said when they reached the south border of the property. He continued down the street until he could turn around.

On their second pass of the property they came up empty.

"Let's head back to town," Howard said.

He turned west onto Hobart Road and headed for Highway 214. On either side of the narrow, paved road the trees gave way to fields of hay or strawberries. The houses were closer to the road, making them easier to see. Large, two-story farmhouses with barns behind them were quickly dismissed since a young woman, on her own, would not be able to afford such a place. Instead, Howard and Dominic were looking for something smaller.

When they reached Quarry, Howard slammed on the brakes causing Dominic to lurch forward in his seat.

"Hey!"

"Sorry," Howard said, bringing the car to a stop on the shoulder of the road. "Is that her?"

Dominic looked out his window. Just as Carolyn entered a small cottage. He looked at the address on the mailbox beside the car door. 13789, it read.

Howard pulled into the dirt driveway and parked.

"Well, this is it," he said before opening his door.

Dominic opened the car door and stepped out onto the grass. The house was small with a brick chimney on the west side, facing the dirt drive. In front were two windows and between them, on either side of the concrete front steps were two brick planters with purple asters. Howard walked up the steps and knocked on the door. Dominic stayed on the narrow walk, since the porch was too small for two people to stand.

Carolyn opened the door. "Oh," she gasped at seeing Howard. "What are you doing here? How did you know where I lived? Are you stalking me?"

"No, no," Howard said. "Nothing like that. We just happen to be headed back to the station and were passing by and saw you. So, I wanted to stop and see how you are."

She looked at the two and cocked her head. Dominic thought she was trying to make up her mind about them.

"Fine, please come in." She stepped back into the house and held the front door open.

Howard opened the screen door and went inside. Dominic followed.

The front door opened directly into the living room that was small but large enough for a loveseat against the wall opposite the window and a television in the corner between the red brick fireplace and the front window. Behind them, to the right of the front door was an equally cozy dining room with a round breakfast table and four matching wood chairs.

"Cute," Howard whispered.

Dominic nodded, not knowing what to say. There were no pictures on the walls, not even a lamp on the side table at the end of the loveseat. Sparce was the word that came to his mind.

"Please, have a seat," she said, directing them toward the dining room.

"Thank you," Howard said.

"Would you care for some coffee?" she asked while they stood by their chairs. Howard stood between the wall and the chair that faced into the living room. Dominic stood with his back toward the window, looking into the kitchenette.

"Sure," Howard answered for them. "That would be great."

"Sit down," she said and took two steps into her cute kitchen. The room was large enough for one cook. An old '50s refrigerator sat to the right of the doorway. Beside it was a double sink beneath a window. Across from the door was a stove with cabinets on either side and above.

"I would have phoned but I didn't get your number," Howard said.

"Oh, I don't have a phone, yet. They wanted a huge deposit and…well, I can't afford it just yet. Do you take cream or sugar?"

"No, thank you. Black is fine."

Dominic began to feel uneasy, as if he were the third wheel on one of Howard's dates. He pulled out a chair and sat down.

Carolyn returned with two mismatched coffee cups and set them down on the table. She then went back in the kitchen only to return with yet another style cup. She sat down across from Dominic.

"Mmm, this is good coffee," Howard said after taking a sip.

Dominic wasn't sure if he was being honest or buttering her up. He took a sip from his cup. It tasted okay.

"I'm glad I noticed you outside," Howard said. "I wanted to check to make sure you were all right."

"I'm okay," she said.

"Have you heard from your brother?"

"No." She shook her head and bit her lower lip. "Can you tell me who was killed?"

"I'm sorry, it was Cody."

Carolyn took in a sharp breath and began nodding her head. Dominic noticed the tendons in her neck tighten as though she were pressing her tongue to the roof of her mouth. He began to feel guilty about not being able to tell her where her brother was.

"Are you okay?" he asked her.

She nodded and drew a deep breath, then slowly let it

out.

"Did you know him well?" Howard asked.

"Not really, he was Samuel's friend," she answered and shrugged.

"May I ask you a question?"

"Shoot—sorry."

"Do you know if Samuel has a car?"

"No," she answered and shook her head. "It's not allowed. If you have a car then you could leave."

"I see," Howard said. "He does have a driver's license."

"Yes. He had to get one for his job driving a tractor. Why?"

"We found out that Mr. Jacobson had a Ford Ranger pickup. It's missing."

Carolyn's eyes widened. "And you think that Samuel took it?"

"Is it possible?" Howard asked.

"No. Not a chance. Samuel wouldn't take anything that didn't belong to him. That was beat into us as children. One time, when Sam was around six or so, mom had a bag of suckers on top of the refrigerator. She used to give us one after school. This particular day, she wasn't there when we got home from school. So, Sam got a chair and got us both a sucker. When mom and that ass-hole got home, she noticed the chair was beside up to the fridge. She knew then what happened and told the ass-bite. He beat us both with a leather strap. I couldn't wear a dress to school for weeks because of the bruises on my legs. Samuel had trouble sitting down. I don't know how he managed at school."

"How awful," Dominic said.

"We survived."

"You shouldn't have had to *survive* your childhood. That's not right."

"But we didn't know better. Different times," she said with a shrug.

"So, Samuel wouldn't take the truck. Do you recall

seeing it?"

Carolyn shook her head again. "No. I can't say as I do."

"What about Mr. Coffey?" Dominic said.

"You'd have to ask him, but I wouldn't bet on him giving you a truthful answer."

"I see." Howard said. He glanced at Dominic and then back at Carolyn. "You don't like him. May I ask why?"

Carolyn looked at him and took a deep breath. She faced Dominic. "I'm sorry, I know I'm not supposed to hate anyone, but I hate him and wish he was dead."

"I see."

"No, you don't," Carolyn said and shook her head. "I take it you met Jane, the little girl in that house?"

"Yes."

"Well, she's *my* daughter."

"Your—"

"Yes. She's mine. I gave birth to her after *daddy* raped me one night."

"I'm so sorry," Howard said.

"I turned seventeen on the day I found out I was pregnant. I planned to run away. I waited until they went to the store, but mom forgot her purse and caught me before I could. We had a little meeting and I was told I was too young to raise a child. They would raise the baby, end of discussion.

"When she was born, they filled out the birth certificate but instead of putting my name on it, he put my mother's."

"But isn't that illegal?" Dominic asked.

"Yes, it is," Howard said. "But it's up to an attorney and the court to straighten out." He looked at Carolyn. "I truly am so sorry."

Carolyn turned away. She looked at her living room. Dominic and Howard exchanged glances.

"When did you move out on your own?" Dominic asked.

Carolyn's head turned back sharply. She looked at him.

"I didn't move out. I was thrown out when I turned eighteen. Luckily my aunt on my real father's side lived a mile away and she took me in. She died last year and I found this place."

"What about Sam? Did they he get thrown out?"

"Not a chance."

"What do you mean?" Howard said.

"There's no way he would do that. Sam wasn't allowed to leave. He was supporting them."

"How was he supporting them?" Dominic asked.

"That lazy bum of a stepfather was injured on his job. He went on disability. Sam's senior year he made him quit school and get a job. When he didn't earn enough, he made him get a second job. He was working two jobs, seven days a week and turning over his paychecks to them."

"So, Mr. Coffey doesn't work?" Howard said.

"Not that he'll admit to. He does mechanic work in that big garage out back of the house. It's all under the table so it won't interfere with his social security checks. I'd turn him in if I knew who to report him to."

Howard nodded his head. Dominic didn't have any answer. He knew nothing about social security other than he had a card.

"So, who said Sam was thrown out?" Carolyn asked.

"Mr. Coffey," Dominic answered.

She shook her head. "He's such a scum bag liar. Cody was the one who convinced Sam to move out. He snuck his things out of the house a couple days ago. He told me he and Cody found a place where the rent was cheap. I figured they moved somewhere in town."

"Actually, they were living just up the road in Mr. Whitaker's old house," Howard said.

"Really?" Carolyn said, looking at them in shock.

"Yeah."

"And that's where…"

"Yes," Howard said.

"But where's Sam?"

"That's what we're trying to find out." Howard reached into the pocket of his coat. "Here's my number. If you hear from him, call me."

"Uh-huh." Carolyn said.

"Do you have a number I can call you at?"

"Just my landlady's. She lives in the house across the driveway." She stood up and grabbed a pen from a kitchen drawer. She tore off a piece of paper from something on the counter and wrote on it. "Here it is," she said, handing it to Howard. "She goes to bed after the news at seven, so call before then if you need."

Howard looked at the number and nodded. "Thank you. Oh, one last question, do you know if Mr. Coffey owns a gun?"

"A gun? What sort of gun?"

"A pistol."

"Yes he does. He has at least two that I know of. He sometimes takes things in lieu of cash. Things he can sell later."

"Do you know where he keeps them?"

"In that garage. Mom refuses to have them in the house. You don't think…oh, God."

"No, we don't think anything yet. We're still trying to sort it out," Howard said.

"I have a question," Dominic said, glancing at Howard. "Is Mr. Coffey right or left handed?"

Carolyn's penciled eyebrows shifted, one up, one down, as she looked puzzled by the question. "He's ambidextrous. Comes in handy as a mechanic, I guess. Why do you ask?"

"Just curious," Howard said. "Well, thank you for the coffee."

Dominic stood up. "Thank you for the coffee. That was very nice of you." He moved toward the front door.

"Do you mind if I check on you from time to time?" Howard asked. "See how you're getting along?"

"Sure," she said.

"Thank you, again." Howard said as he followed Dominic out the door.

Once they were back outside, Dominic, his voice clipped but controlled asked, "What was that all about?"

"What?"

"Wanting to phone her from time to time?"

"I was just trying to stay on her good side so if we need more answers, she'll be willing to help."

"Well, don't lead her on," Dominic said while he opened the car door. "That poor girl has been hurt enough."

CHAPTER NINE

Howard parked the car against the curb outside the Fox Tail Café on the corner of Water and Main in downtown Silverton. It was on the main floor of an old brick building along Restaurant Row, as one newspaper tried to name the three blocks of restaurants had unobstructed views of Silver Creek in back.

"I thought I'd treat you to lunch again," Howard said. He waited for a car to pass before he opened his door and stepped out into the street.

Dominic followed, stepping onto the sidewalk. He looked at the building. He vaguely recalled seeing it before when he was in college. A group of friends had gone to see a movie down the street on the corner of Water and Oak. After the movie they'd ended up here for pizza.

"Oh my," he exclaimed. "I haven't been here in years. What happened to Cloak and Dagger Pizza?"

"Closed down after the owner died a couple years ago. His children didn't want to run it anymore, so they sold it. The new owners changed the name and the menu. It's more of an English pub now."

"A what?"

Howard laughed. "Come on. You'll see." He held the door open for Dominic.

Stepping inside, Dominic felt as if he had been transported to another country and time. The ceiling was clad in dark stained wood that matched the wainscotting. The parts of the wall that were not wood were painted a dark green. Framed lithographs of old paintings were suspended from the picture rail by wire. On either side of the door was the seating area where bare, rustic wooden tables were placed at random. Along the walls beneath the front windows and outer walls was a built-in banquette for seating. Across from the front door was a bar complete with stools bolted to the floor.

"Sit anywhere you like," the barmaid called to them. "As you can see, we aren't busy."

It was true. Only three people were perched on stools at the bar and another couple were seated at a table. Howard directed Dominic to a corner table near the window. He sat down on a chair and motioned for Dominic to sit on the banquette.

Dominic slid along the bench seat until he was directly across from Howard.

"Quite a place," he said. "I can't believe how much it's changed."

"Wait until you see the menu."

Dominic's eyes widened. "Why?"

Howard chuckled. "It's a true English menu."

The barmaid, a stout woman dressed in blue jeans and white blouse with a black apron brought them each a glass of ice water and a menu.

"I'll give you a minute," she said. Dominic had expected to hear an accent but was disappointed that she sounded like a local.

"Oh, that's okay," Howard said. "I know what I want. I'll have the bangers and mash and a pint of O'Doul's."

Dominic frowned at the menu. Nothing was familiar to

him. He looked at Howard for help before turning to the waitress. "I'll have the same. Except, I'll have a cola."

She took the menus and returned to the bar.

"What are bangers and mash?" Dominic asked.

"You'll see," he said. "So, what do you think about the case?"

Dominic relaxed against the wall. "I don't know. We don't have a weapon and we have a missing truck."

"My money is on Samuel, more and more. I think he took the truck."

"I'm not so sure," Dominic said, resisting the urge to tell Howard that Samuel was back at the Abbey in the infirmary, and that he had walked there.

"Before I forget, I'll be right back." Howard jumped to his feet and rushed outside.

Dominic watched him get into the car and use the radio. He imagined Howard was reporting back to the dispatcher, letting them know they'd stopped for lunch.

The waitress returned with two, heavy pottery plates as ridiculously large as the platters used at the Abbey. She set one down in front of Howard's empty chair and the other in front of Dominic. "I'll be right back," she said.

Dominic looked at his plate. In the center was a large helping of mashed potatoes and onion gravy. On top of it were two sausage links the length of a common hotdog but two times as thick. A spoonful of green peas had been tossed on the plate beside the potatoes. Dominic raised an eyebrow.

Howard returned right when the waitress brought their drinks. She placed a tall glass of what looked like beer in front of Howard and an equally large glass of cola in front of Dominic.

"Will there be anything else?" she asked.

"I think we're good to go," Howard said. "Thank you."

"If you need anything, just holler. I'm right over there." She smiled before she left.

Dominic watched as Howard picked up his glass and

took a big gulp. "I thought you weren't supposed to drink on duty?"

Howard looked at the glass in his hand. "This? This isn't alcoholic. It's what they call *near beer*. It tastes like it but won't get you drunk. Here, try it." He held the glass out to Dominic.

Dominic scrunched his nose. "No, I'll take your word for it." Looking at his plate again, he said, "Why don't they just call it sausage and mashed potatoes?"

"Because it doesn't fit with the *ambiance*," Howard said raising his nose into the air. They both laughed.

Dominic took a bite. "So, who did you radio?"

"Susan, down at the station. I asked her to see if she could find the license plate number on the pickup."

"Do you think she can?"

"She's really good. If anyone can, she's the one."

"Once we finish eating," Dominic said. "I think I should get back to the Abbey."

"Oh? Any particular reason?"

"No, I just want to check on a few things."

"Like?"

Dominic didn't want to say. "I want to ask Brother Gregory a couple more questions about Cody."

"Do you want me to come along?"

"No, I'll let you know what he says. I think your being present would be a distraction for him and he might clam up."

"Is he still upset about falling into the fishpond? That was an accident and a lifetime ago."

Dominic laughed. "He still talks about it, but I don't think he's actually upset anymore."

"That's good." Howard shook his head. He picked up his drink and set it back down without taking a sip. "I wish we could catch a break. I mean, my first big case and I feel like I'm losing it."

"You're not losing it. We'll find the missing pieces and

the person responsible."

"I wish I had your optimism. No murder weapon. A missing truck. And the prime suspect or the one person who could tell us what happened is missing."

"Don't worry. You're smart. You'll figure it out. Trust me."

"I do trust you. It's just so damned frustrating."

Dominic grimaced.

After they had finished their lunch, Howard paid the bill and they left. He drove Dominic straight back to the Abbey.

"When you find the license plate number, get the word out," Dominic said as he stepped out of the car. "Let me know if you hear anything."

"I will. Tell Brother Gregory hi for me."

Dominic gave Howard a look. "Sure."

They both laughed.

Dominic watched until Howard's car disappeared behind the gymnasium across the Great Lawn from the Abbey. Then, he then headed inside.

"Hi Jonah, any messages?" he asked the receptionist as he entered the monastery wing.

"A message from Father Anthony," Jonah replied. "He wants to see you. Something about your lesson plan. He's wondering how much longer he's going to have to cover for you."

"Good grief, it's only been two days," Dominic muttered.

Brother Jonah laughed and shrugged.

"Thank you."

Dominic made his way to the infirmary. Sister Mary Francis was at her post. She looked up as Dominic entered.

"Good afternoon," she greeted him.

"Hello, Sister. Any change in our friend?"

"See for yourself." She said, gesturing toward the bed with her open palm.

The curtains on either side of Samuel's bed were pulled

closed leaving the foot of the bed open. The head of the bed was raised to a seating position. Samuel lay on his side in an almost fetal position with his legs drawn up toward his chest. He hugged a pillow tightly while he stared fixedly at the white curtain.

"Samuel?" Dominic said gently while he stood beside the bed. "Samuel?"

Slowly Samuel rolled onto his back and looked at him.

"How are you doing?" Dominic asked.

Samuel's eyes looked Dominic over.

"He's been like this since this morning," Sister Mary Francis said.

Dominic felt pity for him. He wished he knew what to do to make him better. "Has he said anything?"

"No. Not a word. Brother James tried to get him to speak but he can't or won't."

"Has he eaten?"

"Very little. He had a sip or two of soup and a bite of toast, that's all. He didn't touch his breakfast. Brother James said he'll eat when he gets hungry enough, but I'm worried." She looked at Samuel. "Come on, dear boy, talk to us."

Samuel said nothing. He continued to stare at Dominic.

"If you need me, I'll be back at my desk. Brother James had to go to Salem this afternoon. He'll be back in time for Vespers if you need him."

"Thank you, Sister Francis," Dominic said. He waited for the sound of her chair being pulled out at her desk before he turned back toward Samuel.

"Hey buddy," he said. "I suppose you saw what happened?"

Samuel didn't react.

"I know you didn't do it," he continued. "But you have to help me find who did."

Still no acknowledgement.

"It's okay. I'll keep looking. You should rest." Dominic patted the bed beside Samuel.

Samuel looked at Dominic's hand and put his hand over it. Their eyes met for a brief second and Samuel turned away again.

Dominic left the infirmary and headed back to his room. He remembered the ring box he had taken from the house. It was in the top drawer of his dresser. He wanted to take another look at the ring.

Alone in his room, he retrieved the black velvet covered box and sat down at his desk. He turned the desk lamp on and held the box in the glow of the bulb. There were no markings on the box. Carefully he opened it.

A gold band with a half carat diamond was tucked into a single ring slot. Carefully Dominic took it out. He held it closer to the light to see if there were any markings. On the inside of the band was a stamp *14k gold* and a personal engraving that read *Forever*.

Dominic frowned, uncertain of what it meant.

CHAPTER TEN

The next morning, after Mass, Dominic returned to the infirmary. He found Samuel just as he was the day before, staring into space. Dominic wondered if his mind was replaying what he had witnessed.

"Good morning, Samuel," Dominic said, pulling a chair beside the bed and sitting down. "Did you sleep?"

Samuel turned his head, his gaze meeting Dominic's. His blue eyes, usually sharp, now seemed dull. The corners of his mouth dipped slightly. To Dominic he looked like a lost and frightened little boy.

"That's okay, I didn't sleep very well, myself," Dominic continued. "I've been troubled about something I found in the farmhouse." He reached into his pocket and pulled out the small box.

Samuel's eyes followed Dominic's hand and then widened when he saw the box. Dominic was about to open it when Samuel snatched it away from him. He held it to his chest, clutched in one fist and with his other hand over it. Tears escaped his eyes.

"Sam, was that for you from Cody?" Dominic asked.

Samuel did not respond. Tears streamed down his cheeks.

"Sam," Dominic whispered. "I'm so sorry."

Samuel locked eyes with Dominic. With his left hand, he wiped the tears from his cheeks. "He's dead," he said.

The sound of Samuel's voice shocked Dominic. "Yes, Cody is dead."

Samuel turned his head as his eyes glazed over again. He continued to clutch the small box over his heart.

"Sam, whose ring is that?" Dominic asked.

"Mine," he answered.

"Yours?"

"Mine."

Dominic leaned forward and put his hand on the bed. "Did Cody give you the ring?"

Samuel didn't respond.

"Did you see what happened? Did you see who shot Cody?"

Samuel didn't respond.

"Were you there? In the kitchen?"

He shook his head.

"Where were you?" Dominic persisted.

Samuel shuddered. "Upstairs."

A shiver, like a wave of cold water, swept over Dominic and stole his breath. "Oh my," he said. "Did you see who it was?"

Samuel didn't respond.

"It's okay, Sam. You're safe here. No one can harm you."

Even with Dominic's reassurance, Samuel didn't speak, didn't acknowledge him.

"I met your sister, Carolyn," Dominic shifted the conversation. "She's very nice. She's worried about you. Would you like to see her?"

Samuel slowly shook his head but Dominic wasn't sure it was in answer to his question.

"Your mom is worried, too."

Samuel shifted in his bed and turned his back to Dominic.

"I'm sorry, Sam. I didn't mean to upset you more. I'm

trying to find out who did this to Cody and to you. I need your help." Dominic put his hand gently on Samuel's shoulder. Samuel shrugged him off. "Okay, I'll leave you for now. I'll stop back later. I know you didn't do it. Take care, friend."

Dominic returned the chair to beneath the window and left the infirmary. He felt a mixture of hope and fear. At least Samuel spoke, even if only a few words, but at the same time did he make things worse by asking too many questions? He headed downstairs to meet Howard.

CHAPTER ELEVEN

Howard was waiting at the reception desk talking and laughing with Brother Jonah when Dominic arrived. They both went silent when they saw him, making Dominic feel as though they had been talking about him. It was a feeling he hadn't felt since their school days. He still didn't like it.

"So, what's up?" Dominic asked, trying not to sound annoyed.

"Nothing," Howard said. "I was just telling Doug—Brother Jonah here about my time at the police academy."

"What time?" Dominic asked.

"The time in training when we had to chase a suspect and jump a fence. I caught my pants on the fence and tore the seat out right in front of the sergeant who just happened to be the most gorgeous woman I'd ever seen, and who I had a thing for."

"Oh, that," Dominic said, sounding bored. "Shall we be going?"

Howard glanced at Jonah and then at Dominic. "Sure," he answered. "Catch you later Brother Jonah."

"See ya, Detective."

When the two were descending the front steps, Howard

was the first to speak.

"So, what's bothering you, today? Didn't sleep well?"

"I haven't slept well since this whole thing started," Dominic confessed, his tone still tense.

"Gee, Charlie, if you'd rather not—"

"No," Dominic stopped him. "It's just I have a lot on my mind this morning."

"Care to talk about it?"

"I can't," Dominic said. "Not yet."

They both took their seats in the car.

"Burr." Howard shivered. "It's getting colder."

"Fall has arrived," Dominic said. He looked out the driver's door window as Howard drove the car along the road at the edge of the Great Lawn. The trees were pruned and allowed Dominic to see the valley. A blanket of fog concealed the farms and houses below. He felt his mood lighten. "I just love this time of year."

"You've got to be joking," Howard said. He continued to follow the road as it lead them through the forest that formed a barrier between the Abbey and the real world.

"No, I'm serious. I've always loved fall. Oh, I like the other seasons, too, don't get me wrong. It's just that this time of year, with the fog and crisp air, I love sitting inside all snug and warm."

"What would make that even better is having a hot chick to snuggle with," Howard said.

Dominic playfully punched Howard's arm. "Is that all you think about?"

"Sorry, talking with Brother Jonah got me thinking."

"Think about something else. So, what did you do yesterday afternoon?"

"I was busy. Susan located the license number of the truck. We put out a statewide BOLO."

"Have you heard anything?"

"Not yet."

"Say, where are we headed?" Dominic asked when he

realized they were headed out of town toward Meridian.

"That's the other thing I worked on. I got us a search warrant for the Coffey property. Remember you asked Miss Hathaway about what her stepdad does?"

"Yes, he's a mechanic—ah, I see. You think he may be hiding the truck in his shop out back."

"Ding! Ding! Ding! Hand the boy a prize," Howard said with a laugh. "I've sent a few other officers ahead. We'll be meeting them and serving the warrant."

"I'm not so sure we're going to find anything."

"We have to start somewhere. Besides, Mr. Coffey is being a little too cagey for my liking. I think he's hiding something and I aim to find out."

True to his word, three police cars were parked along the side of the road, out of view of the Coffey residence. They waited and then followed Howard's car up the driveway.

Howard stepped out of the car. Dominic did, too.

"You better stay back, Charlie," Howard said. "Let us get started and then I'll bring you in."

"Sure," Dominic said and watched from outside the passenger side of the car.

Howard and four other officers approached the front door. They didn't have to knock. The door opened and Mr. Coffey stood in the threshold.

"What's the meaning of this?" he shouted, as if trying to intimidate Howard and the others.

"We have a warrant to search your house and outbuildings," Howard said and held out a slip of paper.

"For what?" Coffey shouted louder and blocked the entrance.

"Mr. Coffey, please step aside and let my men enter. Otherwise we will be forced to arrest you and take you down to the station."

"You have no right!"

"We have every right. Your stepson is missing and his

best friend was murdered."

"That has nothing to do with me."

"Also, a red Ford Ranger is missing. And you are a mechanic who fixes up old cars or scraps them."

"You won't find anything here."

"Please step aside," Howard said, remaining calm but Dominic could tell he was about to lose it.

Mr. Coffey stepped aside. "Let them through, Sarah," he said to his wife inside the house. As the officers passed by him, he said, "You better not make a mess."

Howard looked over his shoulder at Dominic and motioned with his head for him to come.

"What's he doing here?" Mr. Coffey barked angrily.

"He's assisting us," Howard answered. He stepped into the house.

"Good morning," Dominic said. "I'm so sorry about this."

"Just hurry up and get out."

Howard turned back toward Mr. Coffey. "Where do you keep your handgun?"

"Why?"

"Because we are looking for the murder weapon," Howard said. "If you don't want us tearing apart your lovely home…"

"In the bedroom closet, top shelf. I'll get it—"

"No, we'll get it." Howard turned to one of the officers and told him where to find the gun. The officer disappeared down the hall. A moment later he returned with the revolver in a plastic evidence bag. "Good. Get it to forensics in Salem for testing." He turned back to Mr. Coffey. "Is your shop out back locked?"

"Of course."

"Would you care to unlock it for us? Or would you rather we broke the lock?"

Mr. Coffey's lips thinned to a line and he glared at Howard as he begrudgingly led the way to the shop.

The shop was a converted two-story barn. The main floor, a dirt floor, was packed down and soaked with oil to keep the dust under control. The air reeked making it hard for Dominic to breathe. In the far corner, away from the large main door were old tires. Some were stacked neatly clear up to the loft. Others were just tossed in a heap. A portable work bench and a tall mechanic's tool cabinet on large casters was pulled to the front of an old, beat up, two-door Chevy. The seats had been removed and were piled next to a built-in workbench alone the wall. A makeshift office was built in the corner of the barn opposite the workbench. Howard headed there. Dominic followed closely.

"You won't find a truck in there," Mr. Coffey yelled at them.

In the office was a desk covered with papers and car parts, a grease-stained telephone, and a desk lamp with a cracked, green plastic shade. A four-drawer file cabinet sat behind it in the corner. Two old kitchen chairs with torn upholstery sat across from the desk by the entrance door.

Howard walked over to the desk and began shuffling through the papers.

"What are you doing?" Mr. Coffey said, pushing his way past Dominic.

"Looking for any record of the truck."

"You won't find anything," Mr. Coffey snarled as Howard turned his attention to the file cabinet and pulled open the top drawer. "I tell you, I never saw the truck."

Howard continued to the next drawer and the next. He opened the bottom drawer and straightened up. He grinned and looked at Mr. Coffey. Their eyes met and Mr. Coffey's angry expression turned to a look of worry. Howard closed the drawer. "We're done here," he said. He walked back into the main shop. "Come on, guys. We're through."

The officers and Dominic returned to the driveway. When Howard removed his rubber gloves, Dominic was surprised. He hadn't seen him put them on. They climbed back into the car.

"I told you, you wouldn't find anything," Dominic said.

"Oh, I found something all right," Howard grinned and stared at Mr. Coffey standing on the front steps with his arm around his wife.

"What did you find," Dominic asked.

"His porn stash." Howard laughed and started the engine.

"Oh my," Dominic said, shaking his head.

"We also found a gun, don't forget that," Howard said, pulling onto Meridian and heading toward town.

"It's not the murder weapon," Dominic said.

"How do you know?" Howard said sounding a little annoyed.

"He gave it up to easily."

"We would have found it anyway."

"And because, in order for Mr. Coffey to get to the farmhouse, he would have had to drive. He couldn't drive two cars."

Howard glanced at Dominic and then back at the road ahead. "Damn it!" he cursed and slapped the steering wheel.

"Howard!" Dominic snapped.

"Back to square one."

The drive back to the station was silent. Dominic was lost in thoughts about Samuel. He wanted to tell Howard but he needed to talk to the Abbot first. When they neared the turn off to the abbey, he spoke up.

"Can you drop me off at the Abbey? I need to talk with Abbot Ambrose about something."

"Sure," Howard turned off the main road and headed through the trees. "I can wait for you."

"Actually, it may take a while. How 'bout I call you?"

"Okay, I'll be at the station. Make it before lunch and we can grab something."

"I'll try," Dominic said.

CHAPTER TWELVE

Standing in the hall outside the Abbot's office, Dominic felt his pulse racing. He took a deep breath and knocked on the door.

"Ave," Abbot Ambrose called out from inside.

Dominic opened the door.

"Ah, Dominic," the abbot said with a warm smile. "Come in. Have a seat." He motioned to the chairs in the lounge area. Grabbing his coffee cup, he left his desk and moved to his chair.

Dominic took the remaining chair.

"How's the investigation going?"

"It's sort of hit a wall."

"Really?"

"Howard is grasping at straws. Without the murder weapon he has no other leads."

"I see." He took a sip from his coffee cup and set it down on the wooden coaster on the small table between them.

"Abbot Ambrose, I need to ask if I may have your permission tell Howard about Samuel?" He looked at his superior and held his breath.

"Do you think it would help?"

He exhaled then said, "I'm not sure. Last night when I went to see Samuel, he managed to say a word or two. I think he's coming out of it. Perhaps he could tell Howard what happened?"

"What if he can't?"

"I'm not sure," Dominic said.

"Samuel came to us for sanctuary."

"I'm not sure Howard would see it that way. He may think we're harboring a fugitive or trying to hinder a police investigation."

"I'm not concerned with that," Abbot Ambrose said with a kind smile that didn't reassure Dominic. "Before we can tell Detective Miller, we need Samuel's permission."

"Okay—I mean, yes, Abbot Ambrose."

"Let's go see him."

Abbot Ambrose rose to his feet. Dominic did the same. He followed his superior into the hallway and across the foyer to the monastery wing. Neither said a word.

Once they reached the infirmary, Abbot Ambrose paused for a moment and adjusted the large, gold cross pendant on the chain around his neck before entering.

"Good morning, Abbot Ambrose," Sister Mary Francis said, rising from her chair.

"Good morning, Sister. How are the patients this morning?"

"Father Blaise isn't doing as well today, I'm afraid."

"Any thought as to how long now?"

"It could be imminent," she said. She hastily made the sign of the cross. "Brother Alpheus is doing better. He hopes to return to his duties in the next day or two."

"Splendid. What about our young Samuel?"

"He hasn't spoken, yet. I did manage to get him to take a couple sips of some soup broth, but he's still not eating enough."

Abbot Ambrose nodded. "Very well. Has Brother James

returned from the college dorms? I heard about an accident with one of the seminarians and a ladder."

"No, not yet."

"Very well. I'll just look in on Samuel."

Dominic smiled and nodded as he passed by Sister Mary Francis' desk. She returned the silent greeting.

The curtain was still pulled closed, hiding Samuel's bed from view of the other patients, but more importantly from the curious eyes of visitors. Abbot Ambrose paused at the foot of the bed and looked at Samuel. From where he stood, Dominic could see that the head of the bed was again raised and Samuel was sitting up. He looked at Abbot Ambrose with a stoney expression.

"Good morning, Mr. Hathaway," Abbot Ambrose greeted. "Are you feeling better?"

Samuel's eyes shifted to see Dominic standing beside the abbot. He looked back. "Yes." His voice was faint, a raspy whisper.

"Is Sister Francis treating you well?"

"Yes."

"Splendid. I have a question for you and would like your answer. Brother Dominic has been assisting the police with their investigation. I've kept you out of it to give you time to regain your senses. Are you able to tell me, what happened?"

Again, Samuel's eyes turned to Dominic and then back to the abbot. He took a deep, quivering breath and his eyes began to tear.

Abbot Ambrose walked beside the bed and took Samuel's hand. "It's okay, my child. No one and nothing will harm you here. You are safe."

Samuel's head bowed. He said something but Dominic only caught fragments of what he said. He watched as Abbot Ambrose nodded.

"You realize, you will need to tell the police."

Samuel's eyes widened and he began to tremble.

"It's okay," the abbot said. "The detective is a dear friend of mine. He won't harm you. He needs to know what you saw."

Samuel sat still, staring blindly at the foot of the bed. Slowly he nodded his head.

"Very good, my child," Abbot Ambrose said. "I will let him know you are here." After giving Samuel a blessing, he turned around to leave.

Dominic stepped aside and then returned to the foot of the bed. "I'll stop back later, okay?"

Samuel didn't respond.

Once they were back in the hall outside the infirmary, Abbot Ambrose turned his attention to Dominic.

"You may inform Howard that Samuel is here. Make sure he understands that we are looking after him as he sought sanctuary. He may question him, but he will not be leaving here."

"Yes, Abbot Ambrose," Dominic said, bowing his head in respect. "May I ask what he said?"

"You may," the abbot answered, raising an eyebrow. "But I will leave it to him to tell you."

"All right," Dominic said. "I should call Howard right away. Telling him is going to be awkward. He's bound to be upset that I didn't do so on day one."

"I'm sure you will be fine. If he has any questions, tell him to come see me." Abbot Ambrose smiled and winked. "I'll be in my office."

Dominic waited until the abbot was out of sight before he headed down to the reception desk to phone Howard.

Spurred on by news that Dominic may have a break in the case, it didn't take long for Howard to make the one and a half mile trip from the station to the abbey. He parked his car in the lot by the gym and ran across the Great Lawn. Dominic was waiting at the foot of the steps beneath the portico.

"That was fast," Dominic said.

"You said on the phone you have something big for me?" Howard said, trying to catch his breath.

"Yes," Dominic said. "Let's sit down."

They walked to the side of the steps and sat on the flat, concrete and brick banister. Howard's breathing returned to normal quickly.

"What is it?" he asked.

"I wanted to tell you on day one, but I couldn't."

"Tell me what?"

Dominic averted his gaze to the ground, fearful of Howard's reaction. "Samuel is here in the infirmary."

"He's what?" Howard's voice was raised and amplified by the portico above their heads.

"He showed up before you phoned. He was barefoot, with scratches and torn and soiled clothes. He was in shock and not able to speak. Abbot Ambrose had Brother James take him to the infirmary. When you phoned, we had no idea there was a connection between him and what happened."

"But when you found out—"

"Abbot Ambrose said we couldn't tell you because Samuel came to us for sanctuary. He made me promise not to say anything."

Howard looked at Dominic. "So, I've been running around for two days looking for the killer and you guys have been harboring him?"

"He's not your man."

"How do you know that?"

"Because, he—"

"Don't you even tell me you questioned him without me present."

"No, not that he would answer. I just asked him if he was there. He nodded that he was. Abbot Ambrose spoke with him a few minutes ago. He said it was okay for you to visit the infirmary and ask Samuel what you want."

"I'm not happy about this, Charlie," Howard said. "I thought you were helping me."

"I am."

"Withholding evidence in a murder case is a serious crime."

"Are you going to arrest me?"

Howard pursed his lips and glared at Dominic. He let out a huff and shook his head. "No. I just wish you would have told me sooner is all."

"Me, too. Come on. Let's go see him."

They stood up, walked up the steps, and entered the foyer. They bypassed the reception desk and took the marble stairs to mezzanine. They crossed over to the monastery wing and headed for the infirmary.

"Hello, Sister Francis," Dominic said when they entered.

Sister Mary Francis lowered her brow when she saw Howard.

"This is Detective Miller from the police. He's here to talk with Samuel."

"Miller? Miller? Didn't you go to school here?"

"Yes," Howard answered. "Ages ago."

She nodded and wrote something in her log book. "I remember you, Mister Miller."

"Is that good or bad?"

She gave him a look that answered his question. He tiptoed away.

The curtain around Samuel's bed was pulled back. The head of his bed still raised. From his seated position he had a view of the infirmary. He watched as Dominic and Howard approached.

"Hello Samuel," Dominic greeted.

Samuel didn't respond. He stared at Howard.

"This is my friend, Howard Miller. He's a detective with the police. He's trying to find out what happened."

"Hi Sam," Howard said and held out his hand.

Samuel glanced at it but didn't move.

"I'd like to ask you a few questions. Is that okay?"

Samuel nodded.

"Did you see what happened?"

A head shake but no words.

"Were you there?"

A nod.

"Samuel, it's okay. Please, talk with him. Tell him what happened," Dominic implored. "He's here to help."

Samuel studied Dominic's face before turning his attention to Howard. He still didn't appear trusting of the detective, but his mouth opened.

"Okay," he whispered.

Howard's shoulders relaxed. "You said you were there, where were you?"

"Upstairs."

"Did you hear anything?"

"Yes."

"What?"

"Gun."

"Did you see who it was?"

"No." Tears began to fill Samuel's eyes. His hands gripped the top of his blanket, pulling it to his chest in a wad.

"What happened? Can you tell me?" Howard asked. He sat on the edge of the bed so as not to appear intimidating.

Samuel's mouth contorted as he struggled to regain his composure. Tears began to slip from his eyes. He made no move to wipe them away.

"I...I...heard...shot...I...froze...footsteps...running...door.. ..slam...tires...gravel...he's dead." Samuel began to hug his blanket as his tears turned into sobs.

"What did you do then?"

"Ran."

Howard looked up at Dominic. His eyes were damp. Dominic shook his head as if sympathizing with them both. Howard turned back to Samuel.

"I'll let you rest. Is it okay if I come back to see you later?"

Samuel didn't respond.

Howard patted the blanket beside him and stood. "I'm so sorry. I'll find who did this."

The two left the infirmary.

"So, what do you think?" Dominic asked as they walked down the hall to the stairs.

"I don't know. I need him to talk me through what happened but I agree, judging by his condition, he probably didn't do it. So, I'm back to square one."

CHAPTER THIRTEEN

Sitting at a table away from the other customers at the Markum Diner outside of town, Howard was still brooding over the lack of progress in the case. He picked at the bun on his burger and ate a couple fries. Dominic felt uneasy eating his burger.

"So, what have we learned so far," he said to Howard. "We've ruled out Samuel as a suspect and once you get the ballistics report on Mr. Coffey's gun, you will be able to rule him out as well. That leaves us with the neighbors."

"Or the person who stole the truck. That could be anyone," Howard said. "It's no use, I'm not cut out to be a detective."

Dominic set his cola glass down on the table and let out a huff. "Stop feeling sorry for yourself and focus on the case. It's not about you."

Howard's head recoiled as if he had been slapped in the face. "I never said it was."

"Really? Then what's all this, *woe is me* attitude, and *I'm not cut out to be a detective* nonsense, hmmm?"

Howard looked into Dominic's angry eyes and smirked before laughing. "All right, all right. I give," he said.

"So, when will you get the report about the gun?"

"I submitted it for a rapid test, so I'm hoping to have it by tomorrow."

"Great! Now, who do we have for suspects?"

"We have Mr. Hodges, Mr. Jacobson—"

"You don't seriously think he would kill his own son?"

"According to FBI reports approximately fifty-five percent of all violent crimes are committed by someone known to the victim, and about twelve percent of those are committed by family members. So, I can't rule him out just yet. Just as we can't rule out Coffey even though we didn't find the missing truck. He could have had an accomplice."

"You really think so?"

"I don't know. Anything is possible," Howard ate a couple fries and took a drink of his cola. "I think," he said while still chewing. "I will request a search warrant for the Hodges', the Jacobson's, and the VanDyke's farms."

"I thought you ruled out the VanDykes?"

"I want to test all of their handguns. So, no one is ruled out."

"Okay," Dominic said. "I guess we *are* back to square one."

"Eat up," Howard said. "I need to get the warrants submitted."

Dominic watched as Howard picked up his burger and began eating.

After they finished their lunch, Howard drove them back to the station where he submitted the paperwork for the search warrants. It was four in the afternoon when he received word from the judge. The warrants were approved. With papers in hand, Howard and Dominic left the station.

"I want to do this one first. It's going to be the hardest," he said handing Dominic one of the warrants.

"The Jacobsons?" Dominic said. "Yeah, it's going to be tough. Just be careful the way you word it. That you are trying to rule them out. That you aren't accusing them."

"Don't worry," Howard said as he headed for the Jacobson farm. "I'll be sensitive and gentle."

Howard parked his car in the driveway next to the house and the two of them stepped out. The late afternoon air was a bit chilly, causing Dominic to shiver. He followed Howard up the front steps to the door.

Margaret answered the knock. She smiled but Dominic could see from the glassy look in her eyes, she had been crying. "Boys," she greeted them. "Please come in."

"Thank you, Mrs. Jacobson," Howard said and stepped into the foyer. Dominic followed giving Margaret a brief embrace. "We just stopped by to see how you and Mr. Jacobson are doing. Is he around?"

"Yes, I'm afraid he's left the harvesting to the workers these past few days. He's not been himself since…Well, come into the kitchen. Would you like something to drink, coffee, lemonade?"

"No, we're fine. We really can't stay long," Howard said while they followed her to the kitchen.

John was seated at the kitchen table. His hands cradling a steaming cup of coffee. He looked up at them when they entered. Dominic noticed the dark circles and red around his eyes. From appearances, he guessed Mr. Jacobson wasn't sleeping much either.

"Have you found who did this to my boy?" he asked, his tone sounding gruff but tired.

"Not yet, but we won't give up until we do," Howard answered. "Part of our investigation is trying to eliminate…" He glanced over his shoulder at Dominic as if asking for help.

"Mr. Jacobson, you mentioned that you own a handgun?" Dominic said.

"Yes," he answered with a nod.

"May we see it?" Dominic asked.

"Sure, why?"

"We've found many people on farms have guns and we

are checking them all. What do you use it for?"

"Nothing really. It was my father's. It hasn't been fired in…" He looked at his wife.

"Don't look at me. You know how I feel about those things."

"Well, in ages. I'll go get it."

"Mind if I go with you?" Howard asked.

John's thick, dark, eyebrows lowered as he looked at Howard. His eyebrows suddenly raised and his expression changed to shock. "You don't think—" His tone sounded angry. "Fine! Come on, Detective."

Margaret looked at Dominic. "He doesn't think John had anything to do with…"

"No. We just need to rule out that your handgun wasn't the one that was used."

"What?" John's voice thundered through the house. "Fine. Take it. But I better get it back."

A moment later both John and Howard returned to the kitchen. Howard had a plastic evidence bag with the old revolver inside. John walked across the room to Margaret.

"What's the matter?" she asked.

"He thinks I shot our son."

"No, I didn't say that," Howard said. "I merely asked if I could take the gun to have it tested."

"Yeah, like I have a choice?" He held up his fist with a slip of white paper crumpled in it.

"I promise you, we don't think you had anything to do with Cody's death," Howard said. "We just need to test all the handguns of people he knew."

"Oh dear," Margaret said, putting her hand over her mouth. "You think someone he knew killed him?"

Howard looked at her but Dominic spoke first.

"It's likely. In over half of violent crimes such as this, the assailant is known to the victim."

"Do you think that boy, Samuel, was involved?"

"No," Howard answered much to Dominic's surprise.

"He may have witnessed it but he's still in shock and not talking. The brothers at the Abbey are looking after him."

"Oh dear," Margaret said and put her arms around her husband.

"I will return this as soon as I can, Mr. Jacobson," Howard said. "I promise."

John didn't say a word.

"We should be going," Dominic said.

"Detective Miller," Margaret said. "How soon can we have the funeral?"

"That's up to the coroner, but I'll check with him and have him notify you."

"Thank you."

Dominic and Howard showed themselves out. Back in the car, Howard drove to the next stop, the VanDyke's farm. A uniformed officer was waiting for them when they arrived. Having him present facilitated a smooth retrieval of the handgun. Both Mr. and Mrs. VanDyke were understanding and cooperative.

As Dominic, Howard, and the officer walked across the street toward the Hodges' residence, Dominic leaned closer to Howard.

"What if he's hocked the handgun already?"

"Then he'll need to take us to where he pawned it. But, we'll burn that bridge when we come to it."

Dominic shook his head and smirked at Howard's mixed up metaphor.

The sun had nearly set. The sky toward the west was bright orange, red, and yellow. A cool breeze was starting to blow.

Howard knocked on the front door. Martha greeted them with a questioning smile.

"Good evening, Mrs. Hodges," Howard said. "Is Mr. Hodges home?"

"Yes, he's just finishing his supper. Won't you come in?" She opened the screen door wide and stepped back into the foyer.

The three entered the house. Dominic closed the screen and front door behind them.

"I'll go fetch him," Martha said. She disappeared into the back of the house.

A moment later, Mr. Hodges came walking out. It was obvious by his body language that he was not pleased being called away from his meal.

"What do you want?" he demanded.

"We have a search warrant for your handguns," Howard said holding out the slip of paper.

Mr. Hodges snatched it out of Howard's hand and opened it up. He squinted as he looked it over.

"Where do you keep your handguns, Mr. Hodges?" Howard asked.

"I have them upstairs, I'll go get them."

"No," Howard said, stopping him. "Tell us where they are and the officer will retrieve them."

"This is my house!" Mr. Hodges shouted.

"Yes, and that is a search warrant that gives us permission to search every nook and cranny of your house and property for the handguns. If you don't want us trashing your beautiful home, then tell us where we can find them."

Mr. Hodges looked at the paper then glared at the three of them. "Fine, but don't tell the Mrs. You'll find one in the top drawer of the nightstand in the master bedroom. The other one is on the top shelf in the bedroom opposite the master. They're both loaded, so be careful."

Howard looked at the officer who nodded and then headed up the stairs.

"Mrs. Hodges doesn't like me to keep guns in the house. If she knew I snuck them in here, there'd be hell to pay."

"I understand," Howard said.

A moment later, the officer returned to the foyer and held up two evidence bags each with a gun inside.

"Thank you for your cooperation," Howard said. "We'll get these back to you as soon as possible."

"You better not damage them."

"We won't. They will be tested to see if one of them was used in the shooting."

"Well, I can tell you right now, neither of them was."

"We'll be in touch," Howard said and ushered the other two out the front door.

Once outside, Dominic let out a heavy sigh. "That went better than I had imagined."

"Yeah, I thought for sure he had disposed of the guns," Howard said. He looked at his watch. "Get those to forensics tonight," he instructed the officer and waited for him to leave. Turning to Dominic he said, "Since we've missed your dinner, do you want to grab a bite with me?"

"Sure, but not too late," Dominic said.

CHAPTER FOURTEEN

It was nine o'clock by the time Dominic made it back to the Abbey. Abbot Ambrose was waiting in the foyer for him and by the look on his face, he was not pleased.

"I'm sorry I'm so late," Dominic said, hoping to soothe his grand-uncle's mood.

"Come to my office," he said and led the way.

Once they were alone, he sat down in his customary chair by the floor lamp and Dominic took his seat. The light in the office was dim, which added to a calming atmosphere.

"Is Detective Miller making any progress in the case?"

"I think so. He's trying to rule out suspects."

"Like Mr. and Mrs. Jacobson?"

Dominic looked surprised.

"Mrs. Jacobson phoned me after you left. She was very upset and wanted to know why Howard would be accusing them of killing their own son."

"But—"

"I'm not sure allowing you to assist him is really a wise decision."

"Abbot Ambrose, no one suggested that the Jacobsons had anything to do with Cody's death. Howard merely wanted to test their guns to rule out that they had been used. He collected guns from the neighbors and the Coffeys as well."

"I see," Abbot Ambrose said and nodded. "Sounds like he's grasping at straws."

"Yes, it does. But if none of the guns come back as the murder weapon, then that tells us it was probably a stranger or they disposed of it."

Abbot Ambrose's eyebrows raised. "I see," he said. "Son, I think I will have to withdraw my consent to allowing you to assist Detective Miller."

"But we're so close to having some real answers." Dominic felt panic stirring. For the first time, he realized he was enjoying helping Howard with the case. It was exciting and new.

"*He's* close. This is a matter for the police," Abbot Ambrose corrected. "Your duties are here. I'm concerned about your spiritual welfare. You missed twice and when you are there, I notice your thoughts are miles away. It's come to my attention that you have not been sleeping. Brother Christopher who has the cell next to yours says he hears you pacing at night and sees your light on well into the early hours of the morning."

"It's true. I haven't been as focused as I know I should be, and I have been having trouble sleeping—"

"That is why I think you should resume your classes and leave this investigation to the police."

"But, Abbot Ambrose, Cody was a friend. He was like family."

"Precisely. This has struck too close to home."

"Please, Abbot Ambrose, give me until the end of the week. Surely by then Howard will have a better handle on the case. Just two more days, then I shall resume my classes."

Abbot Ambrose eyed Dominic silently, which made Dominic more nervous and anxious. He stifled the urge to plead his case more, realizing if he did, his superior would not agree to his request. The abbot's expression softened.

"I'm not without a heart, son. Mr. Jacobson was a dear, dear friend to me, too."

"Please," Dominic pleaded.

Abbot Ambrose took a deep breath and began to nod his head. "Very well, I will give you until Sunday, that is three more days, and then you need to return to your duties."

"Thank you," Dominic said, feeling relieved. "May I ask how Samuel is doing?"

"He's asking to see his sister, I believe you know how to reach her?"

"Yes," Dominic answered.

"Very well, please get a hold of her and let her know she may come to see him."

"I will."

"You best get some rest. I'm sure Mr. Miller will be here bright and early tomorrow?"

"Yes, Abbot Ambrose," Dominic said as they stood. "Thank you so much."

"Just remember, Dominic. This is a police matter. You are only an observer."

"Yes, Abbot Ambrose."

Dominic slipped out of the office and waited until he was in the foyer before taking a moment to exhale. He rolled his shoulders to release the tension in them.

Back in his room on the second floor, Dominic pulled out his notebook and flipped the pages until he spotted what he was looking for. He picked up the receiver of his phone and dialed the number written down in his book. The sound of a ring once, twice and then an answer.

"Hello?"

"Good evening. This is Brother Dominic from Saint Michael's Abbey. Is this Miss Hathaway's landlady?"

"Yes."

"Would it be possible to speak with her?"

"Certainly. I'll go get her."

Before Dominic could say anything, he hard the receiver being set down. In the distance he heard what sounded like a screen door slam shut. Several minutes later, there was the sound of the receiver being lifted.

"Hello?" Carolyn said.

"Hello, Miss Hathaway. This is Brother Dominic from Saint Michael's."

"Oh, yes. How are you?"

"I'm fine, thank you. I'm sorry it's late but I have some news for you. Samuel is here at the Abbey—"

"What's he doing there?"

"He showed up here the morning of…it's a long story. He is in our infirmary and he's asking to see you."

"Infirmary?" she repeated. Dominic could tell she was unfamiliar with the word.

"He's in our in-house hospital ward. He was in pretty bad shape when he arrived. It's only now he's been able to speak."

"Was he shot?"

"No, just dehydrated and in shock. But he's asking for you. Can you come tomorrow afternoon?"

"I have no way to get there from here."

"I'll talk with Detective Miller and see if we could pick you up."

"Really? You'd do that?"

"Yes," Dominic said. "Shall we say at one?"

"Okay, I'll be ready."

"Wonderful. See you then."

"Bye."

Dominic heard her hang up before the line went dead. He replaced the receiver and began writing some more notes in his book.

At eleven, he looked up at the clock above his desk and glanced at the wall he shared with Brother Christopher. He turned off the light and went to bed, though he wasn't sure he would be able to sleep. His mind was too cluttered with questions and thoughts about the day. Still, he had to be quiet and give the appearance that he was sleeping. The last thing he wanted was Christopher going to the abbot again.

CHAPTER FIFTEEN

The next morning, after Mass, Dominic waited for Howard by the gymnasium. He didn't want to take the chance of having Abbot Ambrose change his mind and forbid him to continue the investigation. As his nervousness rose, he began to pace while he watched the road coming up through the trees.

After what felt like an hour, Dominic sat down on one of the benches between two large planters. Each planter held an ornamental dwarf cherry tree with purple asters at their base. Father Fiacre, a retired botany teacher, was in charge of the many gardens around the abbey. With his vast knowledge of plants and flowers, which he eagerly conveyed to anyone who complimented his flowerbeds, they were always interesting if not beautiful, and ever changing as he kept up with the seasons.

The sound of an approaching car brought Dominic out of his thoughts and to his feet. He caught sight of the vehicle when it rounded the last corner on its approach to the abbey. It was Howard. Dominic moved to the lawn and raised his hand as though hailing a taxi. The car came to a stop at the edge of the lawn in front of the gymnasium. Howard rolled down his window.

"What's up?" he asked.

"I'll tell you later," Dominic said. He walked around the front of the car and took his place in the passenger seat.

Howard rolled up his window and made a U-turn, heading back the way he had come.

"So, are you going to tell me why you were waiting by the gym instead of the front steps of the Abbey?"

"Because last night Abbot Ambrose called me to his office. He's worried about my involvement with the case. He received a call from the Jacobsons, after we left them. He's concerned that it's detrimental to the abbey's reputation and feels that I need to focus on my duties and let the police handle the case."

"That's crazy. You can't quit now when we're so close to finding out who did this."

"I know. I had to beg him to let me stay on with you. But he's given me until Saturday midnight. After that, you are on your own."

"But that's only three days. I won't get the ballistics reports on the guns for a month."

"A month? Can't you have them speed it up?"

"I submitted it with a rush, but…three more days? I can't solve this without you."

"Yes, you can," Dominic said. "And there's something else."

"What?"

"Samuel wants to see his sister. I called her last night and told her he's asking for her. She doesn't have a way to get here and I sort of said we'd pick her up."

"Oh brother. Now I'm a taxi driver?"

"I figured if we took her to see Samuel, we could tag along and see what they talk about. He might say more to her than what he said to you."

Howard tilted his head back as if thinking about it. Rocking it forward again, he said, "I think that's a good idea.

When?"

"After lunch."

"That's even better," Howard said. "I want to do some more hunting for that truck. No one has reported seeing it. So I'm guessing it must be somewhere around here."

"Where do we start?"

"I was thinking we could check out the wrecking yard outside Silverton. That would be a great place to dispose of it quickly."

"True."

Howard turned south onto highway 214 and headed toward Silverton. Rusty's Auto Yard was located west of Silverton on Paradise Rd. Howard was almost a regular customer. He had visited the yard many times while restoring his old 1970 Cadillac DeVille. It took him several years to find all the parts he needed and still it looked and sounded rough. Dominic found it hard to carry on a conversation while riding in it.

Howard took West Main Street out of town. Once they passed Westfield Street, the scenery went from urban residential to rural. Green rolling hills and oak trees with leaves changing to golds and reds were on both sides of the two lane road. A half mile later, Howard slowed the Town Car and turned right onto Paradise. They passed through a wooded area and the wrecking yard came into view on the right.

Rusty's was set back off the road in a dell. Despite the trees that surrounded it, the yard was still visible. Howard turned off the road and onto the gravel driveway. A cloud of dust formed behind the vehicle as Howard swerved to miss the potholes. There was a big thud when one of the car's tires dropped into a hole.

"Damn it!"

"Howard!" Dominic said.

"Sorry. It just angers me that Rusty doesn't keep his driveway up."

"It drums up business," Dominic teased but Howard failed to see the humor.

After a few more sharp movements, they passed the last of the chuckholes and the road widened to a parking lot. An eight-foot-high metal fence blocked the view of yard. Parallel to the fence, old railroad ties had been placed to stop vehicles from hitting it. Howard parked the car near the main gate, stopping far enough away to avoid scraping the underside of the car on the railroad tie.

They both stepped out of the car at the same time. Dominic had never been to Rusty's or any wrecking yard for that matter. He had only seen them in movies and wondered how reality compared to the Hollywood version.

"Come on," Howard said. He led the way through the open gate.

An old metal jobsite trailer was placed several yards away from the gate. At the top of three wooden steps was a door with an "Open" sign in the window. Dominic followed Howard inside.

The interior of the trailer was divided into two rooms, the customer side and the office side. Shelves along the walls of the customer's room were stocked with auto parts, some new and others used. It was all confusing to Dominic. Howard walked up to the counter that divided the two spaces.

"'morning, Officer," the short, pudgy man in a black knit cap greeted Howard. He wore a clean pair of denim coveralls.

"'morning, Rusty," Howard said. "Only now it's Detective."

"Detective? I'm impressed. A promotion?"

"Yeah, in title only, unfortunately."

"Still looking for Caddy parts? I have some good ones that came in on an old El Dorado."

"No, thanks. I'm actually here on business."

Rusty cocked his head and looked past Howard at

Dominic. "Who's your friend?"

"Brother Dominic from St. Micheal's. He's helping me with a case."

"A monk and a detective," Rusty snickered. "Strange combination."

"Yeah," Howard said. "Say, have you taken in an old red Ford Ranger in the last few days?"

Rusty thought for a moment, his eyes darting from left to right and back again. "A Ford Ranger, you say?"

"Yep."

"Accident?"

"No."

"Towed in?"

"It's possible but I'm looking for more of an owner relinquishment."

Slowly, but not convincingly, Rusty began to shake his head. "Can't say as we have."

"Mind if I take a look around anyway?" Howard asked.

"I would never refuse a potential customer," Rusty said with a hearty laugh that ended in a raspy cough.

"Thanks," Howard said. He turned around and motioned with his head toward the door.

"Nice to me you, Mr. Rusty," Dominic said as he started for the door.

"It's just Rusty," he said.

Dominic walked down the steps and waited for Howard.

"He seems nice. Is Rusty his real name?" Dominic asked.

"Nah, it's George. Rusty is a nickname." Howard gestured with both hands toward the old cars lined up like a car lot, rusting away. Toward the back of the lot was a wall of dented and crushed cars waiting to be sold for scrap. "Come on. Let's take a look around."

"But he said they didn't have the truck."

"That doesn't mean anything. It wouldn't be the first time he's lied."

"What?"

"Yeah," Howard said. "He's all about numero uno. If he admitted to having the truck, he knows I'd seize it and he'd be out whatever he paid for it. My guess is, if it's here, he's on his radio to his lot guy telling him to hide it. So we need to step it up."

Dominic followed Howard down the aisle, disregarding the vehicles that didn't fit the bill. When they reached the end of the first row, the aisle turned and headed along the side fence. Howard walked with determination toward the back of the lot, behind the wall of scrap. Dominic had to pick up his pace to keep up.

On the other side of the heap was a huge machine that was used to crush the stripped cars. There was a large claw crane sitting idle that was used to move the crushed heaps. A man wearing coveralls like Rusty's walked out from among the cars.

"You're not supposed to be back here," he called out.

"Detective Miller and Brother Dominic," Howard said, holding up his badge.

"Oh, I see. What can I do for you?"

"Just having a look around," Howard said, keeping his tone evasive.

"Anything in particular?"

"Any Ford pickups?" Howard asked.

"Fords?" the man squinted, repeating the word. "Nope, I don't think we have any of those. People tend to hold onto them."

Howard nodded. "Well, thanks anyway." He turned around and headed back the way they came. Dominic nodded to the lot attendant and followed after Howard.

"Think he's telling the truth?" Dominic asked when they reached the gate.

"Nope, I wouldn't trust any of them to tell me the time, let alone the truth."

"But what can you do?"

"Nothing. If I were to get a search warrant, by the time I get back, they would have it stripped and crushed. I just hope they aren't lying this time. Meanwhile, we'll have to keep looking."

"But where?"

"I'm not sure," Howard said, opening his car door. "I will know more when the ballistics report comes back on the handguns."

"Are you sure you can't speed them up?"

"Depending on their workload…I'll call them when we get back to the office. You ready for a bite to eat?"

"Sure. But I'm paying," Dominic said.

"Okay."

CHAPTER SIXTEEN

It was nearly two by the time Howard and Dominic picked up Carolyn and brought her to the abbey to see her brother. She insisted she got car sick and needed to sit in the front seat, so Dominic rode in the back. He knew what the real reason was and it had nothing to do with car sickness.

Brother James had brought Samuel downstairs to one of the visiting rooms on the main floor of the students wing. The room was cozy. A decorative fireplace on the left wall anchored the room. A green and gold plaid sofa sat with its back to the entry door while two upholstered wingback chairs faced it. A coffee table with a small centerpiece of silk flowers sat in the center. Behind the chairs a tall window framed a view of the Great Lawn in front of the abbey.

Samuel was seated in the chair nearest the fireplace. Dressed in a lightweight, white waffle-weave robe, white pajamas, and socks. The nearly healed scratches and bruises on his arms and face were barely visible. However, he still had that distant look in his eyes.

When Carolyn stepped into the doorway, Samuel raised his head. His eyes teared. Carolyn rushed to him. She wrapped him in her arms.

"Oh, my poor Sammy," she said. "I've been so worried about you. Where have you been?"

"Here," he answered, his response delayed, his expression vacant, as if his brain was struggling to catch up to reality.

"Why did you come here and not to me?"

"Afraid."

"Oh, baby, you didn't have to be afraid. You know I would protect you."

"No…can't."

"Can't what?" She eased her tight hug and pulled the other chair closer before sitting down.

"You can't…" he said, tears dampening his cheeks. He held onto her hand and trembled.

"Honey, what happened?"

Samuel's eyes became distant again. He blindly stared at the floor.

Dominic and Howard walked around the end of the sofa and sat down.

"Samuel," Howard said. "Can you tell us what happened?"

Without blinking, in a monotone voice as if he were in a trance, he began to speak.

"It was late, Cody had gone to Silverton to pick up dinner. I spilled water on my shirt when I was washing the dishes. So, I went upstairs to change. I heard Cody come home. Then I heard someone else. There was a loud bang and I heard someone ran out the front door."

"Did you see who it was?" Howard asked in a near whisper.

Samuel raised his head but his eyes stayed fixed on some unseen spot on the floor. Slowly he nodded.

"I waited upstairs until they were gone. I heard the truck leave. I called, Cody but he didn't answer. I crept downstairs. I was afraid they would come back. Then, I saw him. Blood. Blood." His expression contorted in a mixture of pain and confusion. "I told him to get up. We had to run, but he wouldn't move." Tears began to fall from his eyes. "I was so scared. I ran. I ran. I ran."

"It's okay, Sammy," Carolyn said and wiped his tears with her hand. "You're safe. No one will hurt you. Sissy is here."

Slowly he looked at her. His voice changed to childlike. "He's dead, sissy. He was my best friend. I loved him." The tears continued to fall.

"I know you did," she said, still trying to console him.

Dominic was shaken deep inside. Samuel was the same age as Howard and him but he seemed like a young child the way he was interacting with his sister.

"Samuel," he spoke gently. "Who killed Cody?"

Samuel raised his eyes. He looked at Dominic and then at Howard. His eyebrows pinched above his nose and the corners of his mouth pulled down slightly. He slowly he turned his head and once again seemed lost.

Brother James stepped into the doorway. He was so tall his head nearly touched the header of the doorway. "I think it's time to take our patient back to his bed."

"Yes," Carolyn agreed. "I'll come back to see you later, Sammy." She kissed his cheek, leaving a faint imprint with her pale pink lipstick.

Samuel didn't speak. He let Brother James take his arm and raise him to his feet. Dominic watched as the two left the room. Suddenly Carolyn burst into tears. Howard quickly moved over to the chair beside her and put his hand on her shoulder.

"It's going to be okay," he said.

"What's happened to him?"

"He's still suffering from the trauma of witnessing the murder. It's going to take a while for him to come out of it but he's made huge strides in the last couple days."

"Has he always been that way with you, acting much younger than he is?" Dominic asked, trying to put it as gently as he could.

"I *am* his big sister. Growing up it was always the two of us. Mom was too busy trying to please that bas—, sorry. Whenever he hurt himself, he always came to me to make it better, but I've never seen him like this." Carolyn's tears gave way to anger. She clenched her teeth. "You better find whoever did this. So help me God, I want him to pay."

"We will," Howard said.

They took Carolyn back to her house. Howard saw her to the door.

While he was busy, Dominic resumed his place in the front passenger seat. When he closed the door, the radio squawked and Dominic heard someone calling for Howard. He rolled down the window.

"Howard," he called.

Howard turned his head toward the car. "What?"

"You're wanted on the radio."

That was all Howard needed to hear to free him from his admirer. He said his goodbyes and left her standing on the front steps of her house.

Sitting down behind the steering wheel, he grabbed the mic and pressed the button on the side of it. "Detective Miller here," he said and released the button.

"Detective Miller, an important report just came in for you. Return to the station."

"On my way," he answered. He turned the key in the ignition and started the car. As he backed out of the driveway, he said, "I hope it's what I think it is."

"The ballistics report?"

"Yes. Keep your fingers crossed."

"I'm not superstitious," Dominic reminded him. "So, what were you two talking about on the porch?"

"I was asking her if she has seen the red Ranger."

"And…"

"She hasn't but said she'd keep a lookout."

"That's good."

Dominic could tell that Howard was anxious to find out what report was waiting for him. He drove just over the speed limit back to the station. They arrived in three minutes.

Howard approached the front desk.

"That was fast," Susan said, looking up from her switchboard and radio.

Susan was an attractive woman with curly dark hair pulled back in a tight bun, expressive brown eyes with long eyelashes. She wore her uniform a little tight, whether it was intentional or not, Dominic wasn't certain. What he did know was she was married to a fireman. His picture sat on her desk in plain view of anyone who looked.

"You have something for me?"

"It's on your desk," she told Howard and resumed her typing.

Dominic followed Howard through the gate at the counter and down a short hallway. A door marked with a stick figure sign indicated a shared bathroom at the far end. To the right was a door with the nameplate of the head of the police, while on the left was a doorless opening to a room with a row of desks positioned to face the entrance.

Howard walked to the right and stopped at the last desk next to the wall. The sound of a toilet flushing could be heard, though faintly, from the other side.

Dominic looked at Howard with concern. Howard smirked.

"Low man on the roster," he said before sitting down in his chair.

On top of his desk was a large manila envelope. He quickly slit it open with his silver letter opener that resembled a thin dagger. Not the best thing to have in the office, Dominic thought quietly.

Howard read the slip of paper and when finished he turned it over and then looked in the envelope.

"Well?" Dominic said. "Is it?"

Howard's puzzled expression faded. "It's the report on the Jacobson's gun. Not a match for the one used to kill Cody."

"That's good, isn't it?"

"We already figured out he didn't do it," Howard said. "So, it's kind of a big nothing." He took a deep breath and let it out. "But, I suppose we could take his gun back and let him know."

Dominic cringed inwardly. He didn't want to go back to see them. Not this soon after their phone call to the Abbot. "Perhaps you should do this on your own," he said.

"Not a chance," Howard said. "I need back up."

"I was afraid you'd say that."

"Why? What's wrong?"

"I told you they phoned the abbot after we left them."

Howard nodded.

"Well, I don't want them to call him again. I've already been cut down to three days."

"I see," Howard said. He looked at the paper again. "But this is good news. Legal confirmation that they most likely had nothing to do with their son's death."

"I'm not so sure they'll appreciate that as much as you think."

"Well, it has to be done. Come on, let's go get their gun and take it back."

Howard stuffed the paper back into its envelope and left it on his desk. The pair then headed back out to his waiting car.

The drive back to the Jacobson farm felt a bit uncomfortable for Dominic. He kept imagining being called into Abbot Ambrose's office upon his return to the Abbey and being told his permission had been rescinded. He said a silent prayer that this visit would end on a much more pleasant note.

Howard parked the car in the driveway and together they made their way to the front door. Howard knocked.

While they waited he studied the handgun in the plastic bag. There was no answer. He knocked again. The sound of rushing footsteps could be heard.

Margaret opened the door. As always, she greeted them with a warm smile. "Please, come in." She opened the screen door for them.

Howard nodded his head politely as he stepped into the foyer. Dominic followed close behind.

"Is Mr. Jacobson in?" Howard asked.

"Yes, we're in the kitchen," she said. She closed the front door and then led the way. "John, we have company," she said and stood behind him while he sat at the table.

John looked up from the newspaper that was spread out. His expression told Dominic he was still seething over their last visit.

"Back to accuse me of killing my own son?" he hissed.

"John, please," Margaret said and gave his shoulders a gentle squeeze. "Would you care for some coffee, tea, or lemonade?"

"They won't be here that long," John said, almost daring them to ask for a drink.

"No, thank you, Mrs. Jacobson," Howard said politely. "I just stopped by to return your gun, Mr. Jacobson. And I want to apologize for any misunderstanding. I never meant to make you feel as if I were accusing you of killing Cody. I just needed to eliminate any question that could arise should I be asked in court if I had tested everyone's guns."

John reached up and took the gun from Howard. As he stared at it in the plastic evidence bag, his expression softened. He looked at Howard. "Here, take it. Dispose of it. I don't want it," he said and handed the bag back to Howard.

"But, Mr. Jacobson, don't you need it?" Howard asked.

"For what? I know it's not the gun that killed my son, but it's a reminder of the one that did. I don't want it around."

Howard took the bag.

"I spoke with your abbot," Mr. Jacobson said to Dominic.

"Yes, I know," Dominic said.

"He said we could have Cody's funeral in the Abbey's church. I hope you both will be there."

"Thank you," Dominic said. "I will be there."

"You, too, Detective."

"I'll do my best," Howard said.

"Margaret, why don't you get them something to drink," John said while he folded the newspaper. "And bring some of that banana nut bread you made. I'm sure these boys are hungry."

CHAPTER SEVENTEEN

The next morning, when Dominic came out after Mass to wait for Howard, he found he was already there and waiting for him in the lobby. "You're early," he said.

"We have a break in the case," Howard said.

"You found the gun?"

"No, the truck. Come on." Howard led the way out of the lobby and to his waiting car. Once they were both belted in and headed toward the main road, Howard continued.

"This morning while patrolling the area, one of the officers noticed a truck driving erratically. When he tried to stop the driver, he drove off. The officer kept after him and the driver only stopped when the truck went off the road into a ditch.

"Where?"

"That's the best part," Howard said. "Near the Coffey property."

"What?"

"Yeah. I couldn't believe it myself."

"What about the driver?"

"He was arrested for fleeing. However, when the officer ran the plates, it came up as the truck belonging to Cody. So, he's in deep trouble."

"Where is he now?"

"He's in our jail."

"What's his name?"

"Clifton Murphy," Howard answered while he turned west on East College Street and headed toward town.

Dominic furrowed his brow. "What's his connection with Cody?"

"Don't know yet. I still have to question him."

"What about the truck?"

"It's been towed to our impound yard. I'm having our forensics team go over it.

"Fingerprints?"

"That's the hope. Or any other clue as to how he came to be in possession of the truck."

Howard parked the car at the curb in front of the station.

"You won't be allowed to come with me when I question the suspect," Howard said as the two walked inside. "However, you can watch and listen from the viewing room."

Howard showed Dominic to a small, dark, narrow room with three chairs lined up against the wall, facing an interior window. Dominic was sure the room used to be a closet. He glanced through the window and saw a man seated at a table in the next room. The man appeared to be the same age as Howard and Dominic. His blonde hair was long, about collar length, and mussed. His blue eyes stared defiantly at them. Dominic took a step back.

"Don't worry," Howard said. "He can't see you. He's looking at his reflection. It's called a two-way mirror. You can see through it on this side but on the other side you'd only see your reflection."

"Oh," Dominic said and cautiously took a step further into the room.

"You can sit here. Stay quiet and you can hear what's said in the other room."

"Okay."

"I'll see you later." Howard told him, and left the room.

Dominic sat down and viewed the room next door. The walls were painted plain white with no pictures or wall hangings of any kind. In the center of the room, directly in front of the mirror, was a metal table and four wooden chairs, two facing the mirror, two facing away. In one of the chairs facing the mirror, a man dressed in a blue shirt with the sleeves rolled up exposing his muscular arms sat. He did not look happy. He jerked at the cuffs around his wrists, trying to free them from a metal loop fastened to the center of the table.

The door to the neighboring room opened and Howard entered along with another officer in uniform. They sat down with their backs to the mirror. A third man, dressed in a business suit sat down beside the suspect. After introductions and some legalese, Howard asked his first question.

"Where did you get the truck?"

The suspect stared at him but said nothing. The man's attorney leaned closer to Clifton and whispered something before sitting back up.

Clifton's expression was defiant. "I bought it from a guy."

"When?" Howard asked.

"Yesterday, the day before, I can't remember."

Dominic knew that last part was a lie. Unless this man had serious short-term memory loss, surely he would know when he made such a large purchase.

"Who did you buy the truck from?"

"Don't know."

"Are you aware that the vehicle was stolen during a murder?"

Clifton's eyes widened. "I didn't have anything to do with that."

"So, you did know."

"No." Clifton looked at his lawyer and then back at

Howard. "I heard about a guy who wanted to sell a truck fast."

"Heard from who?"

"Whom," Dominic whispered to himself.

"Some guy who was drinking at The Roadhouse," he answered. "I don't remember his name. He said this guy was in need of money and it had to be a cash sale, four hundred dollars."

"Four hundred dollars for a Ford Ranger? Didn't you wonder why so cheap?"

"I figured it was a beater. I've been looking for a truck because I work in construction, so the condition didn't matter as long as the engine was good. I told him I was interested." He glanced at his attorney who appeared unconcerned.

"So how and where did you make the purchase?"

"First this guy made a phone call. When he came back he said the seller could meet us in the old IGA parking lot. He asked if I had the money on me."

"Did you?"

"Do I look like I walk around with that kind a cash on me?"

Howard and the officer beside him exchanged glances.

"I don't. I needed to run home first."

"So, you met the guy. Didn't you find it odd that you were buying a truck in the middle of the night?"

"Not really. I figured the guy was desperate. That's why I bought it for three fifty."

Again, exchanged glances.

"Did the guy give you a bill of sale or the title?"

"He said he lost the title, and applied for a new one. He said he would call me when it came in."

"Did he give you his name?"

Clifton lowered his brow while he thought. "It was something strange…Sledges…Hedges?"

"Hodges?" Howard asked.

Clifton's expression brightened. "That's it! How did you know?"

"Will you testify to that?"

"In exchange for what?" the attorney asked.

"Not being charged as an accessory after the fact."

"You can't make that stick."

"You'll have to take that up with the D.A. but for now he'll be charged with ORS 811.540, fleeing or attempting to elude a police officer, ORS 819.300, possession of a stolen vehicle, and resisting arrest," Howard answered and stood up.

The attorney wrote in his notebook and then said something to his client.

"I'll testify if you get me out of here," Clifton said as the attorney stood to leave.

"I'll do what I can," he said.

A moment later the door to the observation room opened. Dominic stood up to greet Howard.

"So, how do you think I did?" he asked.

"You did fine. You got the information, and it sounds like a witness to the sale of the truck. That puts Mr. Hodges in the spotlight."

"True, but I will need more to be able to convict him of murder."

The two left the closet and went to Howard's desk. An envelope, like the previous one that contained the ballistics report on Mr. Jacobson's gun, was waiting on the top of the desk.

"Oh," Howard said and greedily snatched up the envelope. "I hope this is good news." He tore it open with his letter opener then reached inside and pulled out a couple sheets of paper.

"Crap!"

"Howard!"

"Sorry," he said and sat down. He held the papers out to Dominic who took them. "The report on the Vandykes' gun.

It's cleared. Not a match for the weapon that killed Cory."

"That's good." Dominic tried to sound positive. "Since we now know that Mr. Hodges was in possession of Cory's truck, it wouldn't make sense if Mr. VanDyke's gun were the murder weapon."

"True," Howard said and took the papers from Dominic. "I'll make a call and see if I can get them to put a rush on Hodges' guns." He picked up the receiver and dialed a number.

Dominic stepped back, giving Howard some privacy. He looked around the office at the other empty desks and wondered who they belonged to and where their owners were. From where he stood, he couldn't make out the names on the nameplates that sat on the corner of each desk.

"That would be great. Thank you," Howard said and hung up.

Dominic turned back to Howard.

"They said they would get on it right away. They were about to start on Mr. Coffey's guns, but said they would set them aside and go ahead with Hodges'."

"Great, so now we wait?"

"Yeah," Howard said. "I need some coffee. Want some?"

"Sure."

"Let's go across the street. They have the best apple strudel."

"I thought you wanted coffee?"

"You can't have coffee without a good German pastry." Howard laughed as they both left the office.

Kitty-corner from the police station was a three story, German Tudor style building with a corner front door that faced the intersection. Above the door was a turret with decorative wooden doors that reminded Dominic of a cuckoo clock. The doors on the third floor were open, revealing wooden carved statues of a German boy and girl on a swing. Dominic had seen it many times before and each time he swore he heard the ticking of a clock.

Howard opened the door and held it for Dominic. Dominic glanced at the sign above the door, Glockenspiel Bakery and Restaurant. Walking into the restaurant, the aroma of freshly baked sweetbreads struck Dominic causing his stomach to growl. He hoped Howard didn't notice.

The interior of the restaurant didn't disappoint. It matched the exterior with exposed heavy wooden beams, cream white walls with dark wooden wainscotting, and a stone fireplace. The tables were covered with white tablecloths that contrasted with the dark walnut stain on the wooden chairs.

A woman, disappointingly dressed in everyday clothes instead of traditional Bavarian attire, greeted them from behind the pastry display case.

"Detective Miller, good to see you," she said with a cheery smile. "Who's your friend? I don't think I've seen you in here before."

"No," Dominic said.

"He's Brother Dominic from the Abbey. He doesn't get out much." Howard teased. "We'll have a cup of coffee and some of your apple strudel."

"Oh, I've got some warm from the oven. Your timing is impeccable. Sit anywhere you like."

She disappeared into the back room while Dominic and Howard found a seat by a leaded glass window. The window wasn't as fancy as the Rose window in the Abbey's church but it was still beautiful with the different degrees of opaqueness forming a honeycomb design.

The woman returned with a tray. She set a cup of coffee in front of each of them and then a plate with the largest serving of apple strudel Dominic had seen to date. It covered the entire surface of the eight inch plate. She gave them each a cloth napkin and silverware.

"Creamer? Sugar?" she asked.

"No, thank you," Dominic said.

"Black is fine," Howard said with a smile. He watched her leave.

"Another friend of yours?" Dominic asked.

"No," Howard answered. "She's married to the baker in back."

"Is this the normal size they give people?" Dominic said looking at his plate.

"No, it's usually a third this size. What can I say, she likes me."

"Howard," Dominic said and shook his head. "So, now what do we do?"

"We wait," Howard said. "We have a witness that puts Hodges with the truck. We know the truck was taken the night of the murder because it wasn't there the next morning. And living next door gives him easy access. We just need to know which gun fired the shot."

"Do you think he was honest about not having any other handguns?"

"If he wasn't, I'll go back and tear his house apart until I find it."

Dominic knew by Howard's tone that he was serious. He silently hoped for Mrs. Hodges' sake that her husband was telling the truth. But there was something still bothering him. Something didn't feel right.

CHAPTER EIGHTEEN

With the investigation on hold until the ballistics report came in, Dominic had Howard drop him off at the abbey. Alone in his cell, he sat at his desk and went over his notes. He flipped the pages, looking for missed cues. Surely there was something he wasn't seeing. After pouring over his notebook, his head felt numb. He closed his book and decided to go for a walk.

Leaving his room, Dominic headed to the infirmary to see Samuel. When he arrived he found Samuel was dressed and sitting in a chair by the window across from his bed. Dominic approached him.

"Hello Sam," he said with a smile, hoping it would keep him at ease.

"Brother," Samuel said and nodded politely.

"It's good to see you up and about. Would you like to go for a walk with me?"

Samuel hesitated for a moment as if thinking it over, then nodded and stood up.

Dominic led the way into the hall.

"Where are we going?" Samuel asked.

"I thought I would show you the cloister garden."

"The cloister garden? What's that?"

"It's the monastery's private garden behind the abbey. It's for the monks."

"Are you sure it's okay for me to go there?"

"Yes," Dominic said. "We're allowed to bring a guest as long as we clear it with Abbot Ambrose."

"And you did?"

"Yes."

They reached the first floor of the monastery wing and Dominic lead him along the hall toward the back of the abbey. He opened the door and held it for Samuel before following him outside.

The cloister garden was another area maintained by Father Fiacre. The leaves on the ornamental cherry trees were beginning to change from a verdant green to a fiery orange. In the beds beneath the trees, Father Fiacre had planted winter pansies of purple with white centers and white, red, and yellow asters. The flowers lined the red brick path that wound its way through the garden.

"Wow," Samuel said. "It's beautiful."

"Father Fiacre does a wonderful job with God's creations," Dominic said. He motioned for Samuel to walk to the left in a clockwise direction along the path. "How are you doing?"

"Better, I guess," Samuel said. "Seeing Carolyn helped." He let out a heavy sigh.

"That's good. Isn't it?"

He nodded. "Did she tell you about Jane?"

"Yes, she did."

"I know I'm not supposed to hate anyone, but I can't help it. I hate him"

"I understand," Dominic said. "And I'm sure our Heavenly Father understands as well. Is that why you moved out?"

"Part of it. The other part was I met Cody. He showed me I didn't have to live like a slave to them anymore. So, I told both my mom and him that I was moving out. That he'd have to find another way to earn a living. We argued something fierce. He tried ordering me to go to my room but I told him exactly how I felt."

"What about your mother? Did she want you to stay?"

Samuel shrugged his shoulders and frowned. "I don't know anymore. She didn't say anything. She never does unless he allows her to speak. Oh God, I hate that bastard—oh, I'm sorry." He put a hand over his mouth and looked at Dominic.

Dominic ignored the remark. "Do you think he had anything to do with Cody's...?"

"I honestly wouldn't put it past him."

"What about your mother? Do you think she would have helped him?"

Samuel stopped and faced Dominic. "How?"

"I don't know, drive him to the farmhouse?"

Samuel shook his head. "No. She can't drive. Never learned how."

"Can you think of anyone else who would have helped him?"

"Not too many people like that—I'm really trying not to cuss."

"I know," Dominic said. "Not many people like Mr. Coffey."

"Yes. But he has one guy that helps him with his car schemes. He's a drunk named Curtis something. I don't know if I ever knew his last name. But he might help him. They're both dishonest, scumbags."

"I see. Would you be willing to talk with Howard, Detective Miller? He may want you to come to the station and make a formal statement."

Samuel's eyes turned away from Dominic and he stared blindly at the tree branches. Dominic waited and said a silent prayer that he would agree. After what felt like several minutes of silent thought, Samuel lowered his gaze.

"I don't know if I can," he said. He looked at Dominic. "Will you come with me?"

"Of course I will. But I may not be allowed in the room when you are giving your statement. But I'll be there."

Another long pause.

"Okay, I'll do it."

Dominic had barely hung up the telephone after giving Howard the news, when Howard came rushing up the front steps of the Abbey.

"I hope you weren't speeding," Dominic teased when Howard entered the reception room of the monastery wing.

Howard's head bobbed and his shoulders raised slightly before he laughed. "I plead the fifth. Where is he?"

"He just went to the restroom."

"Are you sure he's willing to come down to the station and make a formal statement?"

"Yes," Dominic answered. "He said he would."

"Where is he?" a man's voice thundered from the lobby.

Dominic and Howard recognized it immediately. "Call the station for back up," Howard said to Brother Jonah at the switchboard before he rushed into the lobby. Across the room, Abbot Ambrose and Father Mark, the Dean of the high school seminary, appeared from the students wing.

"What is going on here?" Abbot Ambrose demanded.

"My son is here and I want to know where you're hiding him."

"Who is your son?" Abbot Ambrose asked calmly.

"Samuel Coffey. I was told you were holding him here against his will. I've come to take him home where he belongs."

Abbot Ambrose said. "That's quite an accusation. I assure you, there is no one here who does not wish to be."

Leroy Coffey gritted his teeth. "I'll check for myself."

Abbot Ambrose stepped in front of him. "You shall not.

You shall leave here immediately."

"Out of my way!"

Howard stepped forward. "That's far enough," he said with an authoritative tone. "You have been asked to leave. If you do not, you will be arrested and charged with trespassing."

"And who's going to stop me?" Leroy said.

The doors of the Abbey opened behind Mr. Coffey and two uniformed officers entered. Leroy glanced at them but stayed determined.

"Please leave, Mr. Coffey," Abbot Ambrose said.

"I want my son!"

"You have no son, here," Howard said. "Now, leave on your own or in handcuffs. Your choice."

Leroy's eyes squinted as he looked at the three of them. "This isn't over," he said before turning away. The two officers stepped back, allowing Mr. Coffey to pass between them and out the door.

Dominic took a deep breath and let it out. He was thankful Mr. Coffey didn't persist in his determination to search the abbey. He was grateful that Father Mark was standing beside Abbot Ambrose. He was a trained fighter and could easily have stopped Mr. Coffey just as he had stopped Dominic's Uncle Chester all those years ago.

"Thank you, for the back up," Howard said to the two officers. "Stay here for a moment, I may need an escort to the station." He turned back to Dominic. "Go get him."

Dominic left the foyer but a minute later returned. He noticed that Abbot Ambrose and Father Mark had left. Howard was standing with the other two officers.

When Howard saw Dominic, he gave him a confused look. "Where is he?"

"We have a problem," Dominic answered. "He's changed his mind."

"What?" Howard nearly shouted.

"He heard Mr. Coffey and is afraid. He doesn't want to

leave here.”

“But…but—”

“Can you question him here? I mean, what’s the difference where he tells you?”

“We…” Howard stopped and glanced at the two officers. “Hang on,” he said.

Dominic wasn’t sure if that was meant for him or the officers. A second later he found out when Howard turned toward his colleagues. They spoke with each other quietly and Howard turned back to him.

“Can we use one of the visiting rooms?” he asked.

“Certainly, I’ll just ask Father Mark,” Dominic said. He went to the Dean’s office across from Abbot Ambrose’s in the students wing. Father Mark gave his permission but reminded Dominic that he was free to use any of the vacant rooms and didn’t need to ask. Dominic thanked him and returned to the foyer. “It’s okay,” he said and crossed over to the monastery wing. “I’ll see if Samuel will talk to you here.”

Samuel was waiting nervously for Dominic. Brother Jonah had given him a cup of tea which Samuel cradled in his hands while he sat in a chair he had pulled away from the foyer doors. He looked up when Dominic entered the reception room.

“Sam, Howard said he can speak with you here, if you like?”

“Will you be there?”

Dominic shook his head. “I can’t, but I’ll be right outside the door.”

Samuel looked down at the cup in his hands. The tea’s brown-tinted water rippled as his hands shook. He took a deep breath.

“It would really help us find out who did this to our friend.”

Samuel looked up and his shaking calmed. It was as though hearing Dominic refer to Cody as their friend gave him strength. He nodded and stood. He placed the tea cup on the counter. "Thank you, Brother Jonah. I'm sorry I didn't drink any."

"That's quite all right," Jonah answered kindly. He took the cup and set it on the credenza behind him, against the wall.

Together Samuel and Dominic went into the foyer.

"Hi Samuel," Howard greeted him with a smile, extending his hand.

Samuel nodded, eyeing the other two officers, as he shook Howard's hand.

"Don't worry about them, they are with me. Shall we?" Howard held out his hand like a theater usher directing them toward the doors to the students wing.

Dominic led Samuel and the others to a vacant visiting room, two doors down from Father Mark's office. "I'll be right here," he told Samuel and watched as they entered the room and closed the door, leaving him alone in the hallway.

Try as he might, Dominic could not hear what was being said inside the room. Memories of sitting outside Father Abbots' office eavesdropping on the conversation inside came to mind. It wasn't intentional, at first. However in his memory, he thought they could hear the conversations clearly. This time, when he wanted to hear, he couldn't. He began to pace while he waited.

By the time the door opened, and the four returned to the hallway, a little over an hour had elapsed. Dominic was standing with his back against the wall across from the room. His arms were folded over his chest beneath his long hooded scapular. He pushed away from the wall when he saw the door open.

"How did it go?" Dominic asked.

Howard gave him a smirk. "As if you weren't listening."

"I wasn't," Dominic said in protest. "Besides, I couldn't hear a word."

Howard laughed. "It was fine. Samuel here, did an excellent job." He patted Samuel on the back. "I need to be going but we'll talk soon."

"Howard?" Dominic said in protest as Howard and the two officers left.

"So, everything went okay?" Dominic asked Samuel.

"I think so."

"How do you feel?"

"Tired."

"Come on, I'll walk you back upstairs."

The two walked in silence back to the infirmary. Dominic felt a bit annoyed at being left out of the investigation. But another question bothered him, who told Mr. Coffey about Samuel being there? The only person he could think of was Carolyn but she wouldn't give that information away willingly. Suddenly he felt worried. He reached in his pocket and pulled out his notebook. He thumbed through the pages he found her phone number. He returned to his cell and rang her from the telephone on his desk.

"Hello?" the elderly landlady greeted.

"Hello, this is Brother Dominic from Saint Michael's. May I speak to Carolyn Hathaway?"

There was a short pause. "I'm afraid she doesn't want to talk to anyone right now."

"But it's important. Is she okay?"

"No. She's not. She's been beaten up pretty bad."

"Does she need a doctor?"

"No. I'm taking care of her. She'll be fine in a few days."

"Do you know what happened?"

"Some. I took her to see Jane and Mr. Coffey asked her where her brother was. She said she told him she didn't know and that's when he called her a liar and backhanded her. He grabbed her and dragged her into the house. He kept hitting her until she told him."

"Oh no," Dominic sighed. "I'm so sorry. Please tell her that Sam is safe and fine." He heard her tell Carolyn.

"She's relieved."

"I have a question, how did she get home?"

"I drove her. She had me park on the street while she went to the house."

"I see. I think I should call Detective—"

"No, I'll be all right," Carolyn said.

"Miss Hathaway?"

"Yes. Don't tell Detective Miller. I don't want him to see me like this. Please tell Sammy not to worry. I'll see him soon."

The phone clicked then went silent. Dominic put the receiver back on its cradle. He huffed and picked it up again. He dialed and waited with the receiver to his ear.

Susan answered.

"Has Detective Miller returned to the station?"

"Yes, who may I tell him is calling?"

"Brother Dominic."

The connection went silent and then Dominic heard Howard's voice. "Hi, Charlie."

"Hi. You left so quickly I didn't get a chance to talk to you."

"Sorry, I needed to get back to the station."

"I have some news. I just spoke with Miss Hathaway's landlady. She told me that Mr. Coffey beat the information out of Miss Hathaway about where Samuel is."

"He what?" Howard voice shot up. "Is she okay?"

"Her landlady said she is but… So, what happened with Samuel?"

"Nothing much. He didn't see anyone but said the truck was there when he ran out of the house."

"Interesting."

"I'll say. It wasn't there by the time the first officers arrived on the scene."

"Okay," Dominic said.

"Do you think I should check on Carolyn? I mean make sure she's truly okay?"

"If you do, take me with you."

"I'll think about it."

Howard didn't come by to collect Dominic. The hours passed and for the first time since the case started, Dominic was at Vespers. Life seemed to be returning to normal but even through all the prayers, Dominic's mind kept wandering back to the unanswered questions. Tomorrow was Sunday, and his last chance to help with the case. Monday he would be back in class facing his students.

That evening, instead of joining the other Brothers, Dominic stayed in his room going over his notes for the hundredth time.

"Why would Mr. Hodges kill his tenant? It doesn't make sense," he said aloud as he wrote it down in big, heavy letters. "He wouldn't," he answered and leaned against the back of his chair. "It wasn't him." He started to reach for the telephone but noticed it was past midnight. He yawned and decided to go to bed. He would call Howard in the morning after Mass.

CHAPTER NINETEEN

Morning Mass in the Abbey Church, with the sunlight pouring through the stained glass windows casting a rainbow of colors across the congregation always stirred a sense of awe in Dominic. It brought to mind God's promise of never flooding the earth again and gave Dominic a feeling of hope. During communion, he stole a glance as the attendees stepped forward to receive the sacrament. That's when he noticed Howard standing at the back of the church. He wasn't in line or in a pew. He was standing by the door. A feeling of dreadful anticipation grew inside Dominic.

After the close of Mass the congregation filed out. Dominic followed the procession of brothers into the monastery wing, but as soon as he was able to, he slipped away to meet up with Howard, who was waiting in the lobby.

"Good morning," Dominic greeted. "How's Miss Hathaway?"

"Don't know. Didn't go."

"Really?"

"Oh, don't act shocked. I called to check on her and she turned me down. Said she was going to bed and didn't want to see anyone."

Dominic laughed quietly. "I'm sorry," he said but continued to snicker.

"You know, I'm really not the playboy you may think I am," Howard said. "Besides, I have more important news about the case."

"You do? What?" Dominic asked.

Howard tilted his head toward the outside doors then turned and started toward them. Dominic followed. Once they were outside, crossing the Great Lawn and away from the many curious ears, Howard began.

"Late last night I got the ballistics report, or rather a phone call. Neither of Mr. Hodges' guns were used in the murder."

Dominic nodded.

"But you already figured that out, didn't you?"

"I'm afraid so. I mean, why would he kill his golden goose?"

"His what?"

"His paying renter. He had a good thing going with Cody renting the house behind the owners' backs. It was all gravy income for him. He wouldn't kill anyone. It doesn't make sense."

"True," Howard said with an exaggerated exhale. "But how did he end up with the truck? And why?"

"My guess is since he was the one to discover Cody's body, he took the keys and moved the truck so we wouldn't find it. Perhaps temporarily in one of his outbuildings? Then when the coast was clear, he sold it."

"But why would he do that?"

"Perhaps when he saw his scheme had come to an end, he wanted one last paycheck?" Dominic said.

"True. So, who was the guy in the bar that was the go-between?"

"I'm not sure, but it would have to be someone Mr. Hodges trusted."

"His son, perhaps?"

Dominic nodded. "He never did say where his children lived. Perhaps one is still around here?"

"Good point," Howard said.

"So, arrest him?"

"I'll hold off arresting him until we solve the murder. I don't want word getting out and—"

"Although, it could cause the murderer to think he succeeded in getting away with it," Dominic said. "Let down his guard and all."

"That's true," Howard said. "So, are you thinking it's Coffey?"

"Yes. Can you get an arrest warrant?"

"Slow down, Columbo. We don't even know if Coffey's gun will be a match. I won't get the ballistics until Monday evening, or Tuesday, according to forensics."

Dominic glanced back toward the Abbey in time to see Mr. and Mrs. Jacobson approaching.

"Oh dear," he said quiet enough for Howard's ears but not for the rest of the world.

"Good morning," Margaret greeted them with a warm smile. "Lovely sermon this morning."

"Yes it was," Dominic agreed and racked his brain trying to recall what it was about. He came up empty. "How are you both doing?"

"John and I wanted to tell you personally, Cody's funeral is set for Wednesday morning."

"Wednesday?" Howard said.

"Yes, the harvest is finished and it's time our dear boy was laid to rest."

"Have you gotten any closer to finding out what happened?" Mr. Jacobson asked.

"I believe we have," Howard said. "Though, I can't reveal anything at this moment. But an arrest is only a matter of days, now."

"Good," John hissed.

"Now, honey," Margaret said, patting her husband's arm. "Remember the sermon. We have to forgive others if we are to receive God's mercy and forgiveness."

Mr. Jacobson nodded but remained silent.

"We hope you both will attend," Margaret said.

"Of course we will," Dominic said. He looked at Howard for him to agree but he just stood silent. Dominic nudged him with his elbow. Howard winced.

"Yes," he said. "Yes, I'll be there."

"It'll be at ten o'clock," Margaret said.

"We should be going," John said. Dominic could tell he was uncomfortable. He seemed edgy, not making eye contact with anyone. Dominic's heart ached for him.

The Jacobson's continued on their way to the parking lot by the gymnasium where they had left their car. Dominic waited until they were far enough away before he spoke.

"What's the matter?" he asked Howard.

"I don't like funerals."

"Well no one does and if you did, I'd be concerned," Dominic said. "Make sure you are early."

"I'm always early," Howard protested.

Dominic gave him a knowing look.

"Fine, I'll be here at nine o'clock. Now, let's change the subject. Do you think you can get out of your classes for a few more days?"

"No. Abbot Ambrose made it clear that I need to resume my classes Monday."

"But you don't teach all day do you?"

"No, I have two classes a day, the first and second periods."

"So, you're finished by eleven," Howard said. "That means you're free until Vespers."

"I'm not sure that is what Abbot Ambrose had in mind. I still have papers to grade and—"

"You could do that in the evening, simple wimple."

Howard's comment stirred memories of their old high

school English teacher. It was because of him, Dominic wanted to pursue teaching and more specifically, English. The memory of the morning Father Thomas died came to the fore. He had unexpectedly passed away in his sleep. Brother Simon found him after he didn't show up for breakfast. That was the day Abbot Ambrose asked Dominic to take over teaching English, five years ago. Some of Father Thomas' teaching aids—a collection of movie stills from classic books along with charts and grammar cheat sheets—were passed on to him. It made Dominic feel good knowing that a new generation of students would benefit from such a learned man.

"We'll see," he told Howard.

CHAPTER TWENTY

The next morning, during first period, Brother Dominic was hit with a barrage of questions. Rumors spread about Samuel, although the students didn't know his name. Some said he was a fugitive hiding from the police. Others thought he was a homeless man. And still others speculated he was a monk who had escaped from kidnappers. Dominic said nothing to dispel their suspicions.

When the boys couldn't get answers about the mysterious man hiding out in the monastery wing, one of them, seated in the back, raised his hand.

"Master Bauer?" Dominic called on the boy.

The blonde haired boy rose to his feet beside his desk. "Is it true you have been helping the police with a case?"

Dominic looked at the inquiring faces of his pupils. He closed his book and placed it on his desk. He walked around to the front of his desk and leaned against it, facing the boys.

"Yes, I have," he said. "Unfortunately, I can't discuss it at the present. But once it is solved, I will let you know."

"Wow!" another boy in the back row said.

"Now, let's focus on today's lesson." He picked up his book and opened it again.

Second period seemed like a repeat of the first. Dominic really couldn't blame his students. They were young and curious. He remembered being their age. Everything seemed to be a mystery to solve. Part of him wanted to tell them what was going on but the adult in him felt it unwise.

When his classes were finished for the day, Brother Simon met him outside in the hall.

"It's good to have you back," he said. "Father Abbot wants to see you again, in his office."

"Do you know why?"

Brother Simon's face drained of all expression as he turned to face Dominic. "Since when do I question my superior?"

"True. Please forgive me. It's been a long morning."

Brother Simon's head tilted back and he looked down his nose at Dominic. His eyes reflected his curiosity about the statement since it had been only an hour and a half since school began. He straightened his head. "You best be on your way. Don't keep him waiting."

"Thank you, Brother Simon," Dominic said. He walked away, leaving the principal standing outside his office.

Dominic walked straight down the stairs of the students wing to the first floor. The stairwell was empty with everyone in school. Dominic listened to the sound of his footfalls echo up and down as he descended.

Reaching the first floor, he rounded the corner and headed down the hall to Abbot Ambrose's office. It was a walk he had made countless times before and it still caused a flutter of nervousness. He knocked on the door.

"Ave."

He opened the door. "You wanted to see me?"

"Yes, please come in," Abbot Ambrose said from behind his desk.

Dominic stepped into the office and glanced to his left to see Howard sitting in one of the chairs. "What are you—"

"Detective Miller is here to see you," Abbot Ambrose

said. "He has some news."

Howard rose to his feet. "I got the ballistics report back and it's a match for Coffey's gun."

"You did?" Dominic sounded surprised.

"Yes."

"I was just asking Abbot Ambrose if it would be all right for you to accompany me while I make the arrest."

Dominic turned to see his grand-uncle's reaction. Abbot Ambrose simply nodded slightly leaving Dominic wondering if he was giving him permission or simply agreeing with Howard. He looked back at his friend. "And…"

"I explained how much you have helped me and that it was only fitting for you to be there."

Dominic's eyes once again looked at the abbot and then back at Howard. "I didn't do that much."

"Oh, but you did," Howard said.

"I don't know about that."

"In any event," Abbot Ambrose said. "Detective Miller has informed me he wouldn't have solved this so quickly without your help. So, I have given my permission for you to accompany him."

"I don't know what to say," Dominic said while he stood clutching the handle of his leather bookbag.

"Well, you should go," Abbot Ambrose said and smiled beneath his white beard.

Dominic nodded. "Thank you." He turned to Howard. "I'll take my books to my cell and be right back."

"You may leave them here and pick them up when you return," Abbot Ambrose said. "That way you can tell me all about it."

"Yes, Abbot Ambrose. Thank you." Anticipation and excitement grew in Dominic along with a touch of nervousness. He set his satchel down in the chair beside the door.

"Thank you, Father Abbot," Howard said while he

ushered Dominic into the hall.

"Be safe, both of you."

"We will," Howard said, closing the door.

Once in the hall, Howard was quiet. He rushed Dominic into the foyer and then out the front doors of the abbey before Dominic could say a word.

"I can't believe it," Dominic said as they took their seats in Howard's car.

"Neither can I," Howard said. "I wasn't sure he would agree to let you go."

"No, I mean, that the report came back so quickly."

"Yeah, well, about that…" Howard started the engine and put the car in gear. "It really didn't."

"What?" Dominic shrieked.

"I got to thinking about what you said, about arresting Mr. Hodges and letting it be known so the perp would think he got away with murder."

"But—"

"I know, I told a little white lie. We are going to make an arrest. I wanted you there because I know it will upset Mrs. Hodges and you could comfort her."

"Howard," Dominic groaned. "What am I going to tell Abbot Ambrose when I return?"

"Well, we are arresting someone."

"You know what I mean. He's not going to let me go with you when you make the final arrest."

"Well hopefully if the report comes back today, we can do both."

"That's a big if."

"Miracles happen."

It didn't take long for them to reach the Hodges' farmhouse. This time Howard pulled into their driveway along with the marked police car that had followed them. Dominic and Howard stepped from the car and met the uniformed officer.

"Before you say anything," Howard said to the officer.

"I cleared it with the captain. Brother Dominic is here for spiritual assistance to Mrs. Hodges. He's not going to participate in the arrest."

Dominic recognized the officer from the day they discovered Cody's body. He was the one who questioned them about being too close to the victim. He nodded politely at the officer.

"See that he doesn't," the officer told Howard.

"Don't worry," Howard said. "Come on."

Dominic stayed back, walking five steps behind them.

Howard knocked on the front door. It opened nearly immediately. Mrs. Hodges stood behind the screen.

"Good morning," she said, eyeing them with a bit of trepidation. "What brings you back?"

"Good morning, Mrs. Hodges. May we speak with Mr. Hodges?"

"Certainly," she said. "Would you like to come in?" She opened the screen door.

Howard hesitated for a second before entering the house.

Disappointment flashed through Dominic. He wished they had stayed outside to do this. Reluctantly he hurried into the foyer.

"Wayne, the detective is here to see you," she said entering the living room.

Mr. Hodges sat in his chair and didn't move. The television across from him was on.

"Wayne, didn't you hear me?" Mrs. Hodges said, walking over to the TV and turning it off. She turned around and her expression contorted into one of shock and confusion. "Wayne?" Her voice was strained.

Howard rushed into the living room and to Mr. Hodges' chair. He looked down and then up at the officer. "Call an ambulance!"

The officer darted out the door and back to his car.

Dominic hurriedly made the sign of the cross and went

to Mrs. Hodges' side. He looked at Mr. Hodges. His head was slumped forward. He had both hands on the arms of the chair. Howard felt Mr. Hodges' wrist for a pulse.

"I was just in the kitchen fixing him a snack," Martha said. "I was only gone for a couple minutes."

Howard shoved the coffee table back against the sofa. He dragged Mr. Hodges to the floor, careful not to be too rough. He put his ear to the elderly man's chest. Then straightened up and began chest compressions, counting to himself. He tilted Mr. Hodges' head back and cleared his airway before breathing into his mouth. Dominic watched as Mr. Hodge's chest rose and fell. Howard continued to do CPR.

"Oh, Wayne," Martha groaned.

Dominic put his arm around her shoulders and held her close while he said a silent prayer.

The officer returned and began assisting Howard while in the distance a siren screamed. It grew louder every second.

When the paramedics arrived they took over from Howard. His expression told Dominic what he had already surmised.

"It's a bit crowded in here," Dominic said. "Shall we step outside while these men do their job?"

Mrs. Hodges hesitated a moment, her tear filled eyes focused on her husband's motionless form lying on the floor in front of her. She trembled and raised her head. "Yes," she answered.

Dominic guided her around the paramedics and waiting gurney to the foyer and then out the front door. On the porch were two chairs. Dominic led her to one of them and she sat down. She pulled a small handkerchief with lace edges from a pocket in her apron. Dominic smiled. His grandmother used to wear one just like it when they lived on Tam O'Shanter Drive years ago.

"We've been married for sixty-three years," she said. "I

was sixteen and he was eighteen. My parents were against it. I was too young, they said. It won't last. But they consented. We were married right here at Saint Mary's.

"Wayne's parents owned this farm. His father was killed in the Great War. Wayne dropped out of school to help his brothers work it. He only completed the eighth grade, you know. One by one his brothers left until it was just Wayne and his mother.

"We met at a church breakfast. I knew the moment I saw him. After we were married, I moved in here. I looked after him and his mother. When the depression hit, we lost her. I say she died from a broken heart. She never got over losing her husband." She turned her head toward the front door and then looked at Dominic. "He's gone, isn't he?"

"I—I don't know," Dominic said, feeling his throat tightening. "Is there someone we should call?"

"Our daughter lives in Seattle. We have a son who is still close by, but I—"

"Do you want me to call him?"

"No. I hate to say it, but he's not a good man. He drinks too much and he steals. We tried everything to help him but finally we had to let him go. He spent his teen years in the state home for juvenile delinquents and ever since, he's been in and out of jail. Did Wayne tell you Quentin was the one who discovered that poor boy next door?"

"But I thought Mr. Hodges found him?"

"No. It wasn't Wayne. Quentin had been sneaking around the house next door for months. That's why Wayne put up that light and eventually rented it to that young man, to protect it from Quentin. But that didn't stop him.

"That morning, you know, when the boy died. Wayne told me he caught Quentin coming out of the house the night before. He said he told him to leave and not come back."

"Did he?"

"Wayne said he watched Quentin get in a truck and drive off, so, yes."

"He had a truck?"

"I guess. I've never seen it. Wayne just told me. He said that he went next door to check that everything was okay, and that's when he found the boy."

"But he didn't call the police until the morning," Dominic said, sounding confused.

The sudden bang of the screen door slamming shut caused Dominic to look back over his shoulder. Howard was standing behind him. Dominic stepped aside.

"Mrs. Hodges," Howard's voice was just above a whisper and sounded strained.

"That's okay," Martha said. "I already know."

"I'm so sorry," Howard said. Dominic could tell that he truly meant it.

"May I see him?"

"Uh—"

The screen door opened and the officer came out onto the porch. He held the door while the paramedics wheeled the gurney out. Martha stepped forward, stopping them. "Please, may I see him?"

The older looking of the two paramedics pulled the sheet back, exposing Mr. Hodges' head and shoulders. His eyes were closed and he looked as though he were sleeping. She whispered something to him and then kissed his cheek. The paramedic pulled the sheet back up and they continued on their way.

"Do you want me to stay with you?" Dominic asked.

"No, I'll be fine. I'll give Rachel a call now. I know she will come down." She glanced across the street then back at Howard. "What did you want to see Wayne about?"

Howard glanced at Dominic who shook his head. "Oh, it was nothing important. I just wanted to make sure everything was okay."

"That was kind of you," Martha said. "I best give Rachel a call." She gave them each a gentle but brief hug before going back into her house.

Back in the car, Howard started the engine. He backed out of the driveway and onto the street.

"Well, that didn't turn out as I expected."

"No," Dominic agreed. "But I did find out some more information that could be useful. It seems that Mr. Hodges was not being totally honest with us about when he found Cody."

"What?" Howard shouted, shocked and surprised. The car swerved sharply. Howard overcorrected and slowed to a stop on the shoulder. "Says who?"

"Mrs. Hodges. It seems their son Quentin has been snooping around the old farmhouse next door. That's why Mr. Hodges installed that floodlight and why he rented the house to Cody. The night of the murder, he found Quentin coming out of the Whitaker house. Quentin is the one who took the truck. After that, Mr. Hodges went inside and found Cody."

Howard stared straight. "You mean, he found Cody dead and instead of phoning the police, he went back to bed?"

Dominic didn't respond.

"What a cold bastard! What kind of person does that?"

"I don't know. He might have thought his son killed Cody. Mrs. Hodges said Quentin has a police record."

"Does he now?"

"She said he's been in and out of jail."

"For what?"

"I'm not sure. She mentioned he drinks too much and steals things. Perhaps he was surprised to find Cody in the house?"

"How did he get the keys to the truck?"

"We'll need to find him and ask him."

"True. Seems we've been looking at the wrong Mr. Hodges." Howard pulled the car back onto the road and continued toward town.

"Where now?"

"I need to get a new warrant and then we need to find Quentin Hodges."

CHAPTER TWENTY-ONE

Getting a warrant for Quentin's arrest seemed easier and faster than Dominic expected. With his arrest records for repeated larceny, the judge readily signed off on it. Now the task of finding him. Dominic was beginning to lose hope that it would happen before he had to return to the abbey. After all, it was like looking for the proverbial needle in a haystack. Howard insisted it wouldn't take long. Since they knew Quentin was a drunk he had officers checking out the bars and pubs in town and in Silverton. Still, as the minutes ticked away, Dominic began to worry about what he was going to tell the abbot?

At three past four, Howard received a radio transmission, Quentin had been spotted going into Silver Dollar Pub just north of Silverton. Howard turned the car around and headed south on Main Street. The pub was located on the outskirts of town. A police car was waiting along the side of the road. Howard parked in the lot, and the officer pulled in behind him.

Dominic followed Howard and the officer inside the pub. The dimly lit tavern had two pool tables, one on either side of the entrance. Tables with at least two chairs were scattered throughout the rest of the room. Across from the entrance, along the back wall was a large rustic bar. To Dominic it appeared to be made of reclaimed barn wood, weathered, rough, and faded. Two men sat on stools while the bartender, an older woman with short, curly dark hair, wiped the countertop with a damp, white cloth.

"Well, this looks like the start of a bad joke," she said with a laugh. "It's not every day I see a priest, a cop, and a suit come in here."

"Oh, I'm not—"

"We're looking for a man named Quentin." Howard interrupted Dominic.

"He's right…" she turned to point out the man who had been seated at the end of the bar, but he was gone and the side door was closing.

"He's doing a runner!" Howard shouted and bolted after him. The officer was close on his heels. Dominic followed, slowed a bit by his long habit.

Once outside, Dominic spotted Howard heading across the neighboring field. A stout man was running ahead of him but Howard was closing the gap. The officer was gaining on both of them and passed Howard. He tackled Quentin, and the two rolled and wrestled on the ground. The officer, younger and stronger, subdued him. With Howard's assistance he was quickly cuffed and pulled to his feet.

"Quentin Hodges, you're under arrest," Howard said. "Read him his rights."

The officer recited the Miranda rights while the four headed back to the parking lot and the waiting cars.

"Do you understand the rights I have just read to you?" the officer asked him.

"Yeah," Quentin said belligerently, jerking his arm in an attempt to get free.

Dominic was struck by how much he resembled his father—same build, same glare. They could have easily been mistaken for the other.

"I want a lawyer," he spat.

"Fine, we'll get you one," Howard said.

After a bit of a struggle, Quentin finally settled back in the backseat of the squad car. Howard told the officer to take him to Booking and get him settled into a cell. Questioning would wait until an attorney could be obtained.

"Well, that was different," Dominic said when they were alone in the car. "I've seen people run from cops on TV but not in person."

"When people run they only add to their troubles," Howard said. "They compound their charges and upgrade the degree of severity. It's really a dumb move."

"So now what?"

"It's nearly time for Vespers, should I take you back to the abbey?"

"No," Dominic said. "I would like to stay to hear you question him."

"That could be hours."

"Really?"

"Yes, he has to be processed and we have to wait for a public defender."

"I see." Dominic looked away. The clock was ticking and his time to help with the case was running out. He hoped the abbot wouldn't be too upset with him. But they were so close to finding the truth about what happened to Cody.

"I need to make a quick stop," Howard said.

"Where?"

"I want to check on Miss Hathaway."

"Do you think that is a good idea? She told me she didn't want to see you."

"I know, but..." He turned the car onto Hobart. Before Dominic could protest more, they were pulling into her driveway.

"I don't think this is a good idea," Dominic said as the two stepped out of the car.

"I want to make sure she's okay."

"But—"

Howard knocked on the door. It opened and Carolyn stood looking at them in shock. Her right cheek was bruised and her lip, even though she tried to mask it with lipstick, was split and slightly swollen.

"Hi, Miss Hathaway," Howard said. "Uhm, I—we were in the neighborhood and wanted to check to make sure you're okay."

"I'm fine," she said, and seemed slightly embarrassed as she ran her fingers through her hair and pulled it over her cheek in a heart wrenching attempt to hide her injury.

"Uh, that's good."

"Do you need anything?" he asked.

"No."

Howard hesitated. "I guess we'll be going, then." He turned away but stopped. "Are you sure, you are all right?"

The corners of Carolyn's lips curled and she lowered her head. "I'll be fine," she said.

Again Howard turned to leave but stopped. "One more thing, in case you wanted to know, the funeral for Cody Jacobson will be at ten on Wednesday, at the Abbey. If you need a ride—"

"I'll get one," Carolyn said. "Thank you. Bye."

"Bye," Howard said.

"Well, that was painful," Dominic said as the two returned to the car.

"Yes… Yes, it was." Howard shook his head as though to brush away the images of Miss Hathaway's injuries. "That bastard!" he said, then leaned forward and started the car.

Dominic didn't say a word. He agreed with Howard. How could anyone do that to another?

When they reached the station, Susan greeted them. "The public defender is waiting with his client for you."

"That was quick," Howard said. "We'll let them wait for a bit. Is Officer Barker here?"

"Yes, he's waiting in the break room."

"Thanks, Susan." Howard motioned for Dominic to follow him, then led him to the observation room. "I'm going to get Barker and then question Mr. Hodges. You can wait and listen in here."

"Okay," Dominic said. He looked at the three chairs in front of the two-way mirror and decided to take the middle one. From where he sat he could clearly see the attorney. He was leaning his head close to Quentin's and talking. Although he couldn't hear what was being said, he imagined they were discussing the arrest or the theft of the truck. Either way, the defender didn't look pleased.

Howard and Officer Barker entered the room. Howard flipped a switch mounted on the wall and suddenly, Dominic could hear every word that was said. Howard greeted them both and the two sat down with their backs to the mirror.

"Before you get started, I would like to know what the charges against my client are," the attorney said.

"He's been arrested under suspicion of motor vehicle theft, resisting arrest, fleeing, and murder."

Quentin's eyes widened. "I didn't kill nobody. He was already dead."

"Mr. Hodges!" the attorney said sharply.

"It's true. You can't pin that on me."

"Mr. Hodges!"

"Then tell me what happened," Howard said, ignoring the attorney.

"I advise you to keep silent," the defender said.

"But—"

"Silent."

"We could play it that way, but I have enough to file charges," Howard said. Dominic knew from Howard's tone that he was bluffing.

Quentin began to squirm in his chair. "I'll tell you," he blurted. "I was in need of cash. Since my parents refused to help me, I figured there must be something of value in the old house next door."

"I can't defend you if you are going to keep incriminating yourself," the attorney interrupted.

"But it's the truth."

The attorney lowered his voice and leaned closer to Quentin. "I don't care. Shut up."

Quentin shook his head and continued. "When I got to the house there was a car in the driveway with its headlights on. So, I hid in the hedge and waited. That's when I heard a gunshot. I was about to run when I saw a man come running out of the house. He got into the car and drove away."

"Did you get a look at the man?" Howard interrupted.

"When he passed in front of the headlights, I saw him, but I don't know who he was."

"Can you describe him?"

"He was about average height, maybe six foot, stocky. He had short hair. I only saw him for a second. Oh, he had whiskers."

"A beard?"

"Nah, more like he hadn't shaved in a day or so. Oh, when he got into the car, the light came on and I saw a woman in the passenger seat. At first I was afraid she had seen me. I heard her ask the man, 'Did you get him?' He shut the door before I could hear what he said. They drove off south on Meridian."

"What about the car? Did you recognize the make or model?"

Quentin squinted his eyes, looking even more like his father. "It was a '75 Oldsmobile Cutlass, Crimson Red."

Howard and Officer Barker exchanged looks.

"You're sure," Howard asked, turning his attention back to Quentin.

"Positive," he said.

"How can you be so sure?"

"Because I had one just like it. That was my favorite car. Rode like a dream."

"I need a word with my client," the defender said.

"No!" Quentin shouted. "I want to tell him what happened."

"Go ahead," Howard urged.

"When the car pulled out, I noticed the driver had dropped something. I was about to come out of the hedge when I heard a scream from inside the house and then heard someone running away. I didn't see who it was.

"I waited, then stepped out of hiding. I looked at the ground and that's when I saw it. A gun."

A chill came over Dominic. He sat forward in his chair.

"What did you do with it?"

"I'm no dummy. I know about fingerprints and stuff so I wasn't about to touch it. I used a stick and put it under the seat in the old truck with flat tires. Then I locked the door."

Dominic's stomach tightened. He had looked at that truck the day they found Cody's body. He had been standing inches away from the murder weapon.

"Was that it?"

"No. I still needed cash, so I went in through the back door. It was unlocked. That's when I saw the guy on the floor in the kitchen. I could tell he was dead. There was a wallet and keys on the table, so I grabbed them and ran out."

"With the wallet and keys?"

"Yeah. That's what I said." Quentin looked annoyed for a moment.

"So, how does your father come into this?"

"He caught me coming out of the house. He didn't say much or ask what I was doing. He just told me to get lost. When I headed for the Ford Ranger he tried to stop me, but I jumped in and locked the doors. I started trying the keys until I found the one for the ignition. I drove off and laid low for a couple days."

The attorney shook his head, obviously frustrated with his client.

"Would you be willing to testify to all of this?"

"We want a deal," the defender said.

"If you want a deal maybe you should remember cooperation goes a long way."

"Fine, Assuming my client agrees to help you, what can we knock this down to?"

"Misdemeanor theft and resisting arrest."

"I can work with that," he said. "What if he agreed to inpatient rehab and perform community service?"

"I don't know."

"All of his prior convictions were the result of his drinking."

There was a short silence before Howard said. "True. If you can assure me he'll cooperate and testify."

"He will," he said, shooting a look at his client, who again nodded.

"There's one more thing," Howard said gently, turning his head in Mr. Hodges' direction. "I'm truly sorry to have to tell you this way…your father passed away this morning."

Dominic left the room and moved into the hall. He had just found a comfortable piece of wall to lean against when he saw Howard come out along with Officer Barker. He watched Howard give him instructions and then saw him go on his way.

Finally, Howard turned his attention to Dominic who stepped away from the wall and said, "Sounds like Mrs. Hodges told the truth about her son," Dominic said.

"Yes it does," Howard agreed. "I sent Barker to retrieve the weapon. Once he brings it back, I'll get it over to forensics to have it dusted for fingerprints and tested to see if it matches the bullet that killed Cody."

"I can't believe it," Dominic said.

"I know," Howard agreed. "I better get you back to the abbey. Once I get the report, I'll come and get you. I want you there when we arrest that bastard…" Howard's eyes widened and he looked at Dominic. "Sorry."

"No need."

It was after seven when Dominic walked into the abbey. He was about to go to his cell when he remembered he'd left his satchel in Abbot Ambrose's office. Instantly anxiety filled him. He had missed not only Vespers but dinner. He felt like a child about to be disciplined. He stood outside the abbot's door and knocked.

"Ave."

Slowly he opened the door and found Abbot Ambrose sitting in his chair by the floor lamp, reading a book.

"Come in, son," he greeted Dominic. "Take a seat." He closed his book and set it on the small table between the two chairs.

"I just came to get my bookbag."

"Aren't you going to tell me what happened?"

"Uh-h, yes," Dominic said. He closed the door and sat down in the chair by his grand-uncle and superior.

"Did everything go all right?"

"No, not at all," Dominic said. "We went to arrest Mr. Hodges for theft of Cody's truck, but when we arrived we found him dead."

"Dead?"

"Yes. He was sitting in his chair watching TV while Mrs. Hodges was in the kitchen. He must have had a heart attack or stroke."

"Oh dear," Abbot Ambrose said.

"But, that's when everything took a turn. Howard finally got the break he needed. Mr. Hodges didn't steal the truck, his son Quentin had. In fact, Quentin Hodges saw who the killer is and found the gun."

"I see," Abbot Ambrose said, sounding more worried than thrilled as Dominic thought he would be.

"Howard will have the gun tested and then get a warrant for Mr. Coffey's arrest. He said he wants to pick me up before he makes the arrest."

"He does, does he?"

Dominic knew from the tone of Abbot Ambrose's voice that permission was not going to be as easy to get. "I know I've missed Vespers and meals this past week, but it was for a good cause. And now we are just hours away from making an arrest."

"I know, son," Abbot Ambrose said. "I'm worried about you. Are you hearing what you are saying?"

Dominic felt confused. "I don't understand?"

"This is a police matter. There is no *we*. You were only meant to be an observer."

"Yes, I know," Dominic said, feeling defensive but then realizing Abbot Ambrose was right. He had taken a personal interest in the case and ingratiated himself into it. "I'm sorry, Abbot Ambrose."

"I understand. Mr. Jacobson was your friend and you want to see this through, but at what cost? I'm charged with looking out not only for your physical wellbeing but also your spiritual wellbeing. I must say, I am worried."

Dominic simply nodded. He felt ashamed for neglecting his prayers and spiritual duties. At the same time, they were so close to reaching justice. "I'm sorry. You are right. I have been negligent. There is no excuse."

Abbot Ambrose's leaned forward slightly. "I understand, too, that I am as guilty as you. I gave you my permission to assist in this matter. It would not be right for me not to allow you to finish what you started. If Mr. Miller can wait until you are finished with your classes tomorrow, you may go. Then it's back to your students and duties."

"Thank you, Abbot Ambrose. May I go? I have papers to correct before morning."

"Yes," he answered. Dominic rose to his feet. "One more thing, son," Abbot Ambrose said. "I asked Sister Faith to leave you a sandwich in case you were hungry when you returned. It'll be in the kitchen."

"Thank you," Dominic said. "Good night." He started out the door and then remembered his satchel. "I almost forgot." He grabbed his satchel and slipped out the door.

His stomach grumbled. A sandwich and even a glass of cold milk sounded good to him. Dominic headed to the kitchen.

CHAPTER TWENTY-TWO

Dominic took a cold shower the next morning in an attempt to chase away his sleepiness. It was a quarter past two when he finished correcting papers and went to bed. Running on three hours of sleep, his head felt foggy. But he knew he couldn't let Abbot Ambrose see it out of fear he would recommend he take the afternoon to rest instead of accompanying Howard.

At breakfast, he felt as if the shower had done the trick, but then one of the novices began reading from the Bible. The passage was from the Book of Psalms and was beautiful but the young brother read in a dreadful monotone that awakened Dominic's need to sleep. He poured himself another cup of black coffee in an attempt to chase it away.

As the meal continued, Dominic glanced time and again at the head table where the abbot and prior sat. If they could see his struggle, they gave no evidence of it. Instead they ate in silence.

After breakfast, the monks met in the abbey church for Mass with the high school students. The cycle of kneel, sit, stand kept Dominic from nodding off. The lively and animated sermon from the enthusiastic Father Genesius was the remedy Dominic needed. Filled with renewed energy, he headed to his first class after the conclusion if the Mass.

The next two hours flew by. Dominic was anticipating Howard would be waiting for him, so after his last class he rushed to his cell and traded his satchel for his case notebook. He tucked it securely in the large pocket of his habit, and he rushed downstairs.

"Aah, Dominic," Abbot Ambrose said when Dominic reached the lobby. "How are you doing?"

"Fine, Abbot Ambrose."

"Splendid. I wanted you to know that Mr. Hathaway is going to be moving out of the infirmary and into one of our guest rooms. Brother James said he has made a full recovery and no longer needs to be there."

"That's good news," Dominic said. "Does he need any help?"

"No. However, you may want to fill him in on the latest developments in the case. It's only fair he should be told. His sister will be coming later this afternoon to visit him. Perhaps then would be a good time?"

"Yes, it would."

"I believe Detective Miller just pulled up."

Dominic turned around and sure enough, Howard's Town Car was parked at the foot of the steps. "Thank you, Abbot Ambrose."

Howard was opening his car door when Dominic reached the bottom of the steps.

"Oh, you're ready," he said and sat back down in the driver's seat.

Dominic slid into the passenger seat.

"Did you get into trouble last night?" Howard asked.

"No. Not really. Well, a little. Abbot Ambrose said after today I need to focus on my duties and let you handle police matters."

Howard didn't say anything. He just bobbed his head and turned the car around.

"So, how was your morning?" Dominic asked.

"Busy. First thing this morning I took the gun to forensics. They lifted the fingerprints from it and tested it. It was a rush job but it is a match for the gun used. I, then secured warrants for the arrest of both the Coffeys."

"Both?"

"Yes, she was there, too. She may not have pulled the trigger but she was an accomplice based on what was overheard that night."

Dominic was stunned. "What about the girl. Jane?"

"I called family services. A social worker will meet us at the property and take her someplace safe."

"Shouldn't she go with her mother, Carolyn?"

"It's up to the courts and the family service people."

"I see."

"A couple of uniformed officers have been watching the house since last night. We'll meet up with them and make the arrests."

"I can't believe it's almost over," Dominic said.

"This part at least," Howard said. "The rest will be up to the D.A.'s office and the courts. The hope is they will be convicted and sent to jail where they belong. But, don't get your hopes up. I've known cases where everyone knew the person was guilty and still they walked over some technicality or another. It's not what's morally right, it's what's legal."

"They should be one and the same," Dominic said while Howard turned south onto Meridian. "But I understand. Imperfect people equals imperfect justice."

"We'll just have to wait and see."

When they arrived on the street in front of the property, Howard and Dominic stepped out of the car and met the two officers and a woman from family services. The woman was attractive in her white blouse, dark blue blazer and matching skirt. Dominic noticed she was wearing white tennis shoes which he found a bit odd, an unusual contrast to the formal outfit.

"Good morning, Detective. I see you brought a priest?" she said eyeing Dominic. "I hope things will go calmly and not traumatize the child."

"That makes five of us," he answered. He glanced at Dominic. "And he's not a priest. This is Brother Dominic from Saint Michael's. He's been riding along with me during this investigation."

"I see," she said, sounding skeptical.

"Are we ready?" Howard asked.

"Yes," the men responded.

"I'll go to the door first and ask for Mr. Coffey to step out. Hopefully he will comply. Then we'll make the arrest. Once we have him in custody, we will make contact with Mrs. Coffey and that's when you'll come in," he said, looking at the woman. "Once you are there, we'll take Mrs. Coffey into custody." He hesitated a moment, looking at the woman. "May I have a quick word with you before we go any further?"

"Sure," she answered.

Dominic watched as the two went a few yards away and spoke quietly. The woman began bobbing her head as she listened. He recognized her expression of stunned realization. Howard must be filling her in on the family dynamics and who the child's real mother was.

"Thank you," he said when Howard rejoined the group.

"For what?" Howard scoffed. "Are we ready?"

Howard and the two policemen took the lead. Dominic followed at a safe distance with the family services worker. They stopped and stood at the rear of the Oldsmobile, ready to duck down if things went south.

Howard knocked on the front door. To Dominic's relief and dread Mr. Coffey answered. He looked at the three officers and for a split second fear registered on his face. Dominic held his breath.

"What do you want?" he demanded, as though by

sounding aggressive he would intimidate the three trained men.

"I'd like to have a word with you out here," Howard said calmly.

Mr. Coffey pulled the door closed behind him as he stepped out onto the front porch. "What's this about?"

"Turn around and put your hands on the wall, please."

"Why?" Mr. Coffey demanded but complied.

Howard quickly took out his handcuffs and slapped one on Mr. Coffey's left wrist. "You are under arrest under suspicion of the murder of Cody Jacobson."

"What?" Mr. Coffey protested but Howard grabbed his right arm, pulled it back and snapped the cuff around his wrist.

Officer Barker stepped forward and read him his Miranda Rights directly from a small card. At that point Mr. Coffey became silent and was led past Dominic to the waiting police car in the driveway.

Howard knocked on the door again. This time Jane answered the door.

"Yes?" she said, looking around for her father.

"Is your mother home?"

"Yes," she answered, sounding a bit confused. "Where's my dad?"

"Can you tell her Detective Miller would like a word with her?"

"Uh-huh," she started to close the front door but Howard's hand jetted out and stopped it. Jane ran back into the house.

A moment later Sarah appeared at the door.

"Jane said you wanted to see me?"

"Yes, ma'am, would you mind stepping outside, please?"

Dominic was so focused on Howard that he didn't notice the social worker had joined the officers on the porch.

"Mommy?" Jane said following Sarah out the front

door.

The social worker stepped forward and put her hands gently on Jane's shoulders. "Let's go over here," she said and she turned Jane away from the officers and her mother.

"Sarah Coffey, you're under arrest as an accessory to the murder of Cody Jacobson." Howard said. One of the officers handed him a pair of handcuffs and he quickly put them on her while he read her the Miranda rights.

"What about Jane?" she cried, struggling against the officer as she tried to get one last glimpse of the little girl.

"Don't worry about her," he said, while they continued on their way. "Child Protective Services will make sure she is looked after."

"No," Sarah shrieked. "Call Carolyn! She should take care of her."

"I will inform the detective. Watch your head."

Sarah sat down obediently and watched as the door was closed.

"It's okay," the woman said, trying to console a crying Jane.

Dominic walked up to the porch. Howard was standing silently surveying the scene in front of the house.

"I can't believe that went so well," he said to Howard.

"It's not over yet. We may have caught our murderers but we still have to make sure the charges stick."

"I heard Mrs. Coffey say she wanted Carolyn to have Jane. Do you think they will allow it?"

Howard nodded. "They prefer to place children with a family member instead of a foster home. I explained to Mrs. Winters their strange situation and that Carolyn is the girl's biological mother."

"That's good," Dominic said.

"I need to make one more stop before I take you back to the abbey."

"Sure."

After locking the front door, Howard and Dominic

followed Mrs. Winters and Jane to the street where their cars were parked. The two police cars were already gone. They took their places in the front seat of the Town Car. Howard started the engine and made a U-turn before heading north.

Dominic didn't ask but he knew where they were headed. He glanced at the old farmhouse as they passed it. The crime scene tape was still strung around the front of the house and truck. In the driveway next door he noticed a car with Washington plates. He smiled to himself confident that Martha's daughter had arrived.

Howard turned into the driveway of the Jacobson's farm. He parked the car and took a deep breath. "Come on," he said.

They stepped out of the car and made their way to the front of the house. Standing on the porch, Howard knocked on the wall beside the front door. The screen door was latched but the front door was open to allow the autumn air to filter into the house. Dominic tried not to look through the screen but he noticed Mrs. Jacobson approaching.

"Detective Miller, Brother Dominic, what a surprise," she greeted them and unlatched the screen door. "Do come in."

"Thank you," Howard said. "Is Mr. Jacobson in?"

"You know it. He's having a late lunch in the kitchen. Would you boys like something to eat? I made plenty of egg salad sandwiches and my special lemonade."

"Sure," Howard said and they followed her into the kitchen.

"John, we have company," Margaret announced.

Mr. Jacobson looked up from the newspaper. He quickly folded it up and tossed it aside. "Well, welcome. Please, have a seat."

"Thank you, Mr. Jacobson," Dominic said. He pulled out a chair and sat down across the table from him. Howard sat down with his back to the wall and facing Mrs. Jacobson.

"What brings you out here?" John asked.

"I have some news," Howard said.

"Oh my," Margaret said, setting a plate with a sandwich cut in half in front of them both. She went back to the cupboard to retrieve two tall glasses before returning with them. After passing them to Dominic, she took her seat.

"I wanted you both to hear this directly from me," Howard began. "I just arrested the two people responsible for Cody's death."

"Two people?" John questioned.

"Yes, they both had a part in it."

"May I ask who they are?" Margaret said.

"Mr. and Mrs. Leroy Coffey."

"What?" she gasped. "Aren't they Samuel's parents?"

"Samuel's mother but Mr. Coffey is his stepfather," Dominic said.

"What's next?"

"They will be arraigned and then there will be a trial."

John nodded. "How long will that take?"

"The arraignment is pretty quick, within the next day or so. But the trial could take a year or so."

"I see." John looked at his wife and took her hand.

"Thank you," Margaret said. Dominic could see the tears welling in her eyes, glistening as she blinked them away. "Now our boy can rest in peace."

CHAPTER TWENTY-THREE

The morning sun was just over the tops of the trees to the east of the abbey. It cast long shadows across the Great Lawn. Some of the dogwood trees had lost all their leaves and reminded Dominic that fall had definitely arrived. He walked slowly along the sidewalk in front of the abbey. His thoughts were on Cody, not the man, but the young boy full of hope and dreams. He was a gentle boy who was a member of Saint Thomas dorm, thereby escaping Dougary and his thugs harassment that he and Howard had experienced.

After graduation, Dominic lost track of Cody. He heard through the Grapevine—the name Howard had given a group of women at Saint Mary's in town—that Cody had dropped out of college and was working on the farm. It surprised Dominic, since Cody, unlike his younger brother, seemed unsuited for manual labor. Dominic hoped Cody had found some happiness in his short life.

In the distance, the sound of cars approaching reached Dominic's ears. He looked in the direction of the gymnasium. A group of people had gathered and were making their way toward the abbey along the sidewalk that bordered the Great Lawn. Behind them, a black hearse came into view, followed by a black Town Car that looked a lot like Howard's. Dominic turned around and headed back into the abbey.

"They're here," he said to Samuel and Carolyn who were waiting in the lobby.

"We best go into the church," Carolyn said. "I don't want them to see us."

"Why?" Dominic asked.

"I don't want them to look at us and be reminded that it was our mother and stepfather who killed their son."

"Nonsense. You're not responsible for their actions."

"I just don't want to cause them more pain," Carolyn said. "I'll see you inside," she told Samuel and kissed him on the cheek. "Come along, Jane."

"She really does mean well," Samuel said, his eyes fixed on the glass doors.

Dominic glanced over his shoulder. The hearse had stopped at the foot of the steps. Mr. and Mrs. Jacobson and their son Craig were surrounded by a group of family and friends. Some of the women gave Margaret a hug while the men shook hands with each other. One by one they made their way up the stairs.

Samuel stepped back, out of the way to let the mourners pass into the church. He was still watching the hearse intently.

Dominic broke his concentration by saying, "How are you doing?"

"Don't ask. I'm afraid if anyone's nice to me, I'll break down in tears."

"I understand."

Samuel glimpsed Jane wave to him from the doors to the abbey church. When he raised his hand to wave goodbye, a sparkle on his right hand caught Dominic's attention. It was the ring from the jewelry box.

"Nice ring," Dominic said.

Samuel clasped his fingers and looked down at it. "It

was my father's wedding ring."

"Oh."

"It's the only thing I have of his. Mom did away with all of his pictures but kept this. She gave it to me when she gave Carolyn her ring."

"When was that?"

"Right after Jane was born."

The doors to the lobby opened and another wave of mourners entered. Some looked at Samuel with questioning eyes. Others seemed more judgmental. Samuel appeared not to notice. He was still trying to focus on the hearse.

"Brother Dominic," someone in the middle of the crowd called out.

Dominic's head tilted and shifted as he tried to spot who had said his name. The crowd passed and a lone man dressed in a dark blue suit came into view. He had blond hair that was combed neatly and feathered on the sides. He wore glasses that made his blue eyes seem brighter. A slender man, he slipped through the line queueing up at the doors of the abbey church. He laughed at Dominic's confusion.

"What's the matter, don't you recognize me?" he said.

"Gus?" Dominic said in disbelief. "It can't be."

"Yes," he said and laughed.

The two hugged briefly. When Dominic came to live at the abbey's Home for Boys sixteen years ago, Gus had been one of his closest friends.

"Why didn't you tell me you were coming?"

"Because I wanted to surprise you. Howard told me about Cody and I knew I had to come. He was one of the good guys."

"Yes, he was. Say, I want you to meet Cody's closest friend," Dominic said, turning toward Samuel. "Samuel, this is my old friend, Gustav Kugele. I just call him Gus. We were members of Saint Nicholas dorm when we were kids. Oh, the mischief we got into. Gus, this is Samuel."

"Nice to meet you, Gus," Samuel said and held out his

hand.

The door opened again and a gust of cool air rushed in. Dominic turned around. Howard had made it, albeit a little later than nine o'clock, but he was there just the same, and he wasn't alone. Beside him was a thin monk dressed in a white cassock with a black hooded scapular. Dominic recognized Rick immediately. He left Gus with Samuel and greeted them.

"I don't believe it," he said, "It's good of you to come, Brother Conrad."

"I can't believe it either," Conrad said. "What's this world coming to?"

"I told him what happened," Howard said. "I had to. It's a long drive from his monastery to here and he doesn't talk much."

Dominic chuckled. "Well, come see Gus and meet Samuel."

Dominic was overjoyed to be reunited with his three childhood friends. It felt as if no time had passed.

The sound of the church bell tolling, one ring for each year of Cody's short life, reminded Dominic of why they were reunited. Quietly they walked into the abbey church and Dominic left them seated alongside Samuel, his sister, and her daughter. His place was in the choir stalls with the rest of his brothers.

The Mass seemed longer than usual due to the addition of the solemn procession of mourners paying their respects around the open coffin. From his stall, Dominic watched as Samuel made his way toward the coffin and paused. He fumbled with the ring on his finger and wiped a tear from his cheek. He saw Howard nudge him to keep the line moving, but Dominic was sure Samuel's farewell wasn't complete.

After the Mass, the hearse led the way down the hill and to the cemetery at the north end of town. There the four friends and Samuel huddled together. The graveside service was short. Mr. and Mrs. Jacobson and Craig sat in folding chairs to the side of the coffin while the rest of the observers stood.

Dominic noticed that Margaret wasn't fixed on her son's coffin, but on Samuel instead, her expression was unreadable.

When Father Mark finished the last prayer and dismissed everyone with the announcement that the family has invited all in attendance to join them at the abbey for a buffet lunch, Mrs. Jacobson stood up and walked over to Samuel. He looked panicked, but she wrapped her arms around him.

"I'm so happy Cody had a friend in you," she said. "How are you doing?"

He shrugged and looked down.

She put her hand gently on his cheek and he burst into tears.

"It's okay," she said holding onto him while he cried.

"What's going on?" Gus whispered in Dominic's ear.

"Samuel was there when Cody was shot," Dominic said. "Turned out his mother and stepfather were the ones behind it."

"Oh no," Gus groaned. "The poor guy."

In the months and weeks that followed, life had all but returned to normal for Dominic. Samuel moved out of the abbey and in with his sister. The rumors the students were hearing and sharing faded away once the newspaper articles on the murder started.

Since Dominic was a witness to the investigation, he was subpoenaed to be present during the trial, something that distressed Abbot Ambrose when he saw Dominic's picture in the local newspaper and on the evening news. Thankfully the trial lasted only one week.

Sarah Coffey's attorney approached the D.A. with a plea deal. If they would drop the charges against her, she would willingly testify against her husband. After hearing from Carolyn and Samuel about the abuse their mother had endured for years at the hand of her husband, the D.A. agreed. In the end, Leroy Coffey was convicted of first-degree murder and received a life sentence with the possibility of parole after thirty years.

While Dominic sat in his room, his telephone rang.

"Hello?"

"This is Brother Jonah at the switchboard. You have a visitor."

"I'll be right down." Dominic hung up the phone and put his red pen down. Questions about who it could be flooded his mind, after all, Howard knows his direct number and he's the only one he could think of at the moment. He left his cell and went down to the reception desk. "Jonah?"

Brother Jonah looked up from the switchboard. "He's waiting for you on the front steps."

"Thank you."

When Dominic entered the foyer and looked through the glass doors to the outside, he spotted a blonde haired man standing with his back to the doors looking away from the abbey. He recognized him immediately.

"Samuel," Dominic said softly as he joined him on the front steps.

Samuel turned around. His shoulders were raised toward his ears and his hands were buried deep in the pockets of his coat to stave off the chilly autumn air. He smiled when he saw Dominic.

"What brings you here," Dominic asked.

"I came to say goodbye. And to thank you for everything you did."

"That's not necessary, but you're welcome. What do you mean, goodbye?"

"I'm moving to Seattle. Gus was able to get me a job

with the company he works for. I don't know much about computers but I'm eager to learn."

"That's wonderful, but it's a big change from living here," Dominic said, trying not to cast a pall on his excitement. "I mean, Seattle is a huge city."

"I know, I think it's just what I need."

"What about your sister?"

"Carolyn and Jane are getting a place in Salem with mom. Mom sold the house and property. There were just too many bad memories."

"I understand," Dominic said. "Well, I'm happy for all three of you. When do you leave?"

"Right now. I have a taxi waiting for me." Samuel nodded his head toward the gymnasium.

Dominic looked at the parking lot and saw the cab waiting. It's engine running and a cloud of fog rising from the exhaust pipe.

"I shouldn't keep you, then."

"Thank you, again," Samuel said. He quickly and without warning embraced Dominic.

Dominic returned the hug. "Please keep in touch."

"I will," Samuel said and stepped back.

"Go with God's blessing and know that you'll always have a place here."

"Thank you."

Dominic watched Samuel run down the steps and head across the Great Lawn. He wasn't running to the cab so much as running toward his future, Dominic realized.

As Samuel vanished from sight, Dominic turned, exhaled softly, and stepped back into the abbey.

ABOUT THE AUTHOR

James M. McCracken spent much of his teenage years away from his family in a seminary boarding school. It was there that his love for writing began. It is his experiences while at the boarding school that serve as the inspiration for the *Charlie MacCready Mystery* series and the *Brother Dominic & Detective Miller Mystery* series. His writing incorporates elements of mystery and suspense with unexpected twists and is often emotionally resonant with a focus on character relationships and interactions. For more about his books, visit his website jamesmmccracken.com.

James M. McCracken currently resides in Central Oregon. He is a longtime member and president of the non-profit Northwest Independent Writers Association (NIWA) that assists local indie authors. For more information visit their website niwawriters.com.

More Books by James M. McCracken:

A Brother Dominic & Detective Miller Mystery

Murder Close to Home
Murder in the Lighthouse

A Charlie MacCready Mystery

The Ghost in the Attic
Shadows in the Dark
Sirens in the Night
Lost Angel
Lost and Found